Adrianne Beer's work expertly navigates the vulnerability of dating life in Chicago. In "Do You Believe in God? And Other Second Date Questions," a Me Too-ed indie musician interests and then underwhelms a woman who has seen accusations against him on Tumblr. Refreshingly honest, the work steers clear from insisting people fit into discrete moral categories. A millennial Mary Gaitskill, Beer's work is clear-eyed rather than wide-eyed.

— DANIELA OLSZEWSKA, AUTHOR OF
CITIZEN J AND *HOW TO FEEL CONFIDENT
WITH YOUR SPECIAL TALENTS*

In "A Foreign Taste," Lisa Montagne bravely recounts scenes from a marriage that should have never been. Taken in by a seemingly suave Englishman, a very young woman ignores the potential for brutality he clearly telegraphs. This is a courageous contribution to a courageous book.

— TERENCE HAWKINS, AUTHOR OF *THE
RAGE OF ACHILLES* AND FOUNDER OF
THE YALE WRITERS WORKSHOP

The complicated mess of dating and romance comes through in Margo McCall's delightful story, "When I Dream I Die." Reeled in at the opening scene, I couldn't stop reading as this doomed-from-the-start relationship unfolded. Red flags abound and McCall's humorous touches and deft storytelling make for an intriguing, shocking, and memorable story.

— DESIREE KANNEL, AUTHOR OF THE NOVEL *LUCKY JOHN (BLACK ROSE, 2020)* AND THE SHORT STORY *"RUNNING MAN" (RUNNING WILD PRESS ANTHOLOGY, 2019)*. *WWW.DESIREEKANNEL.COM*

"Heart Swindler" involves courtroom drama, lies, and love — or rather, manipulations of love. A page-turner, it is told through the lens of a perceptive juror, raising many questions about what is real or imagined in the land of romance. Aptly titled, this engaging piece reveals an often-invisible crime and sheds light on a dark and twisted tale of love.

— PATRICIA HOOLIHAN, AUTHOR OF *HANDS AND HEART TOGETHER-DAILY MEDITATIONS FOR CAREGIVERS AND STORM PRAYERS: RETRIEVING AND REIMAGINING MATTERS OF THE SOUL WWW.PATRICIAHOOLIHAN.COM*

"I've Been Swindled" by Rebecca Rush is a tilt-a-whirl of a read! I was hooked from the first sentence—the mix of absurdity, acid, humor, and honesty makes so many direct hits. The super-fast pace is almost out of control, just like the relationship between the protagonist and a "famous librarian." I hope at this point that famous librarian is dead of untreated syphilis. Rush rocks!

— LAURIE NOTARO, #1 NEW YORK TIMES BEST-SELLING AUTHOR OF *THE IDIOT GIRL'S ACTION ADVENTURE CLUB* AND FINALIST FOR *THE THURBER AWARD FOR AMERICAN HUMOR*

Writing as Amara Phoenix, Alicia Delory's "Patio" is a stunning piece that reminds us that even during pain and loss, there is humor and light waiting for us if we stay the course...even if what props us up is sometimes crude and shoddy. Delory's voice is one you'll want to listen to again and again. Keep your eyes on this writer – she's one to watch.

— MICHELLE BOYAJIAN, AUTHOR OF *LIES OF THE HEART*

Bobby Rollins' flash fiction "A Lesson in A Minute" may take only a minute to read, but its impact will stick with you for days.

— DAVID LABOUNTY, BLUE CUBICLE PRESS

RED FLAGS

TALES OF LOVE AND INSTINCT

EDITED BY LISA MONTAGNE

RUNNING
Wild
PRESS

CONTENTS

Edited by Lisa Montagne

Published in North America and Europe by Running Wild Press. Visit Running
Wild Press at www.runningwildpress.com Educators, librarians, book clubs (as
well as the eternally curious), go to www.runningwildpress.com.

ISBN (pbk) 978-1-955062-33-6

ISBN (ebook) 978-1-955062-34-3

FOREWORD

THE INTUITION COMPASS

By Lisa Montagne

Like most of us, I have made terrible decisions—some real stinkers, ranging from wearing flip flops for gardening with a rusty hoe to being involved in bad relationships, which appeared fresh but were rotten underneath. The consequences of these dodgy decisions required a variety of remedies from antibiotics to divorce—sometimes both needed to solve trouble caused by men. As a result, I have lots of regrets and many consequences to live with. I love those time-loop movies that give the characters do-overs. I delight in the notion of making things right for myself and my loved ones. "If only," I sigh as the credits roll and melancholy settles on my heart. It would be so convenient to have a time spinner or tesseract in my pocket. Or even a hot tub nearby in a pinch.

Sadly, instead of a time machine gadget, a standard-issue intuition compass is my only equipment for navigating the space-time continuum of life. If there were any justice in this world, an instruction manual for this compass should be issued at birth. But we all know that no manual, warranty nor guarantee of proper functioning comes with this equipment, a flaw in the system beyond our control. So, I have mostly forgiven myself for making bad choices. In those moments, when I was choosing the wrong guy, the wrong city, the wrong school, the wrong job, the wrong doctor, or even the wrong restaurant, I honestly believed that I was making a good decision based on thoughtful consideration. I am not a rash nor stupid person, and I have always valued doing the right thing. But all the good intentions in the world did not prevent me —time and again— from unintentionally bending over to get royally screwed, and not in the pleasant way.

I was born with a lot of confidence. Most people probably are. One short story in this compilation is about me as a 4-year-old who still had the needle of her intuition compass directed at true north. But, the cogs and wheels of my intuition compass got knocked off-kilter along the journey, which drained my confidence like so much lubricant leaking out of a faulty steering system. Despite thinking I found the enlightened path forward, I have often ended up in a frightening, dark Mirkwood full of monsters instead of at a quiet seaside cottage full of kind, nurturing people. But why? Why does this happen to rational, well-intentioned people like me and maybe you? It is partially a matter of losing trust in our natural intuition and failing to follow our best instincts.

Psychologists proffer that intuition is an instinct we are born with, like the adrenaline fight or flight response. But intuition is meant for more subtle situations on a lesser scale than being chased by a lion. Among other things, intuition acts as a stranger-danger alarm and keeps us steered towards survival and hopefully a successful life. As we know, this does not always go as planned. We may be hardwired to assess both larger and lesser dangers, but if a danger is not so immediate, dressed up in glad rags, boosts our flagging confidence, or shrouded in some tantalizing mystery, it may be difficult to see warning flags waving furiously at us through the fog of emotion, excitement, or fear. It's such an easy thing for our intuition compasses to go awry, the needles made crazy by these magnetic hazards. One joke starts with a psychologist asking a patient, "But you recognized the red flags, right?" The patient replies, "I thought it was a carnival."

Warning signals can also be clouded by other elements, such as caring what our community thinks of us, also a survival instinct. I can't say how many times I've made decisions based on what others say. Obviously, not being a dick is generally a good idea if one wants to be accepted in a community, so it's always a good idea to consider the advice of others. Being curious helps us grow. But just because a perceived authority says so does not mean it is the right thing to do. This took me a long time to learn.

I lacked trust in my inner voice for a long time because I was conditioned by society, religion, and gender roles that if someone was older, wiser, male, or even just a cool kid, then they probably knew better than me. At times, I was bullied by these people, letting them spew bilge all over me, then blame me for making the mess. I was their pre-slipper Cinderella, mopping up a situation that had nothing whatsoever to do with me. So even though I was born pretty smart, and I had an innate feeling for what was right and wrong early on, I didn't always make the right moves because the guts of my intuition compass were eaten away by these corrosive agents.

By the time I was in my early teens, I had tucked my head under the collar of a metaphorical overcoat and marched upwind into the gale force of life believing that most other people probably knew better than I did what was best for me. Don't get me wrong. I am the last person to blame others for my mistakes; I'm usually quite the opposite. I'm just acknowledging the many ways people can get knocked off course. Because in the end, me, you, and every damn body are also in collusion with that asshole free will. Sometimes I make choices just because I want to.

Then, there are our mothers if we are lucky enough to have one. Mine was mostly pretty great—well, more interesting than great, if I'm honest. As most mothers do, she meant well. However, she was not much help with how to use my intuition compass because hers was pretty crap itself. She passed on what she learned growing up in the 1940s and 50s: Blend in and know my place in the world as a woman, and then rewards will follow. Although these patriarchal weeds were being choked out by the time I came along, these expectations were still tugging some girls (and boys) under the riptide of oppression, especially in the evangelical church that my mother raised me in. Ironically, with her beauty, bright personality, and keen intelligence, blending in was an impossible task for my mother. She was as subtle as a peacock in a chicken coop. But she wanted for me what she couldn't achieve for herself. So, while she could, she screamed in my face when I wanted to wear boy's clothes or when I frankly commented when one or more of our relatives acted like a creep. Apparently, one shouldn't be honest in earshot of said family, especially when I was the youngest of my generation. I was expected to know my place in the pecking order.

Despite a crap-ton of evidence to the contrary, my mother sincerely believed that people were good, which is admirable to a degree, but her intuition compass lacked a bullshit meter. She was blind to the threats of the church elder who looked down her blouse, the pleasant-looking guy or relative who wanted to "invest" her money, and—her personal favorite—the pyramid scheme salesman. She loved those asshats. An entire underground economy of fraudsters preys on people like my mother. She acted as if a deluge of stranger's candy was always welcome to rain down on our yard—the more the merrier appealed to her gregarious personality. My mother's welcome mat to the world modeled a generosity of spirit that I value to this day. I still cautiously harbor optimism that at least some people, workplaces, education systems, and even my country are good deep down under the layers of muck—despite observing that crap-ton of evidence to the contrary for myself. But my mother's trust in everyone and everything also resulted in a lot of pain, heartbreak, and low bank account balances. Her hoped-for rewards for good behavior usually did not materialize. She suffered. She died relatively young and alone. Her quirky rose-colored glasses served as a smoke screen to prevent me from reading warning signs correctly for years.

By the time I was 18, I had stumbled down the worst path of my life. As I said, my intuition compass was in a bad way by then. I married a divorced man who was in his 30s. My mother let me do it. She was trying to survive my father leaving her for a much younger woman, so she wanted me to have a protector and be married as a virgin, according to the ideals of our evangelical Christianity. I met him through our church pastor. What could go wrong? No really. I honestly believed that I would be treated with love and respect. But it should be no surprise this was the biggest *Nope!* of my life. My intuition compass was woefully incapable of detecting an abusive predator seeking to take advantage of an innocent young girl. When I woke up from that living nightmare four years later, I went to work on repairing my intuition compass. It took a lot of further mistakes, discipline, and focus to put it right again. I wish it had been as easy as stumbling into a time machine, but of course it wasn't. I simply had to put in the work.

Eventually, I got back in tune with my inborn instincts of intuition. It turns out that I may have a higher intuition quotient than most. According to my Meyers-Briggs personality profile, a time-tested psychological instrument that measures traits such as extroversion and intuition, I should be holed up in a Victorian parlor with a turban on my head working as a crystal-ball medium, a role I most certainly don't want nor particularly believe in. My Meyers-Briggs profile is INFJ, an acronym for the traits of introvert-intuitive-feeling-judging, which occurs in less than 3% of the U.S. population. I've certainly been told enough times that I'm *different*. Meh. These days, I lean into it. If you haven't already, I highly recommend looking into what makes your compass tick. It's liberating.

I don't know how it works—*like at all*—but because of the way I'm built, I feel disturbances in the force. Whether I like it or not, there seems to be an invisible thread between me and most people, and not just the ones I'm closest to. Even at great distances, intuitive introverts like me can sense when people are in pain, mad, or sad. And introverts are not necessarily shy. A lot of introverts have a performer gene—I definitely have one. It was well known that Robin Williams was a quiet introvert privately, but a madman on stage. I don't do it on purpose, but people seem drawn to me in public. Give me half an hour and I can strike up a meaningful conversation with just about anyone in a bar. This quality helps me with my roles as a college professor, performer, and event host because these days I can read people at 20 paces, like a sharpshooter sizing up a target. Empathy is a hard-earned substance that keeps my intuition compass well-oiled and functioning. But this particular magnetic quality can also be a gigantic pain in the butt if I'm not careful.

Today, I understand better who my mother was. People were drawn to her, too. She passed away 23 years ago, but dozens still tell me how much they loved her. When I was young, I thought everyone was like me and my mother—open, honest, happy. Unburdened by crippling insecurity, mental deficiencies, or just plain meanness. Obviously, that is not the case. So, I have chosen a different path than my darling mother. I not only protect myself from bad people, but I also protect my schedule because introverts need a lot of time alone to recharge their compass batteries. I need space to fine-tune my senses to discern who deserves my attention and who doesn't. It's not news that one must achieve balance. If I'm too much in tune— or out of tune—with my intuition, I lose my footing on the tightrope of life, like my mother often did.

Nobody's perfect. I still spend too much time worrying about other people, their concerns wired into my sphere like radio waves. I still can't always recognize when somebody has ill intent, is driven by twisted motives, or is a simply a flake. Putting faith in myself first not only vastly improves my quality of life, it also keeps me from being mired in other people's shit. I give no quarter to drama that I'm not forced to by some necessity, such as work or family relations. I also have a handful of friends who are like family. Long-term relationships are bound to have complications, so we strive to smooth over the rough patches. But when I'm not obligated to deal with someone, I live by a three-strikes rule—cross me a third time, and you're kicked to the curb. That's the way it has to be for my sanity, and possibly yours. You should try it. It's exhilarating.

The essays and short stories in *Red Flags: Tales of Love and Instinct* explore intuition and instinct, probing surgeon-like into what happens when one does or doesn't heed the red flags. Some of the protagonists cannot see the red flags, some are the red flags themselves, and some play the knife-edge. All bear witness to the struggles, defeats and triumphs that make up the funny, horrific, strange journey of life.

The authors featured in *Red Flags: Tales of Love and Instinct* are from a diverse range of ages, genders, backgrounds, and professions. Their narratives ebb high and low, oozing vulnerability, shock, honesty, and whimsy as the characters navigate awkward dating moments, dramatic life changes, gaslighting, abuse, struggles with addiction, witnessing fraud, risking adventure, avoiding close calls, surviving the 2020 pandemic, and the vicissitudes of marriage. While most of the characters, settings, and some situations have been fictionalized to both protect identities and serve the narratives, these stories are all based on real situations and profound truths that drive the emotional arcs. My pieces are rooted in real-life events but some details are partially fictionalized as I attempt to bend reality with laser beams of warning or hope.

You can read this book in any order. You don't have to start with the first piece. I dare you to flip to the middle and dive right in. However, you should know that I arranged these essays and stories intentionally to take you on a journey from the familiar and funny to the disturbing and on to a safer harbor at the end.

Today, as I keep my eyes eagle-like on the path ahead to detect signs of warning or danger, I ask myself these questions: Am I listening to myself or to what someone else said? Does what someone else said align with what I truly feel is best for me? Are there any warning flags? What may happen if I ignore these signs? Do I err on the side of caution or take a leap of faith knowing things could all go to poop on the way down? Am I prepared to fix a problem of my own making? Am I prepared not to bitch if things go sideways? Or can I absolve myself, recognizing that it really is not me, it's them?

There is no doubt that making decisions is hard. Hell, the

simplest of daily communications with other people is hard. You can't always get it right, and that's okay. The point is to take agency. Take control. Take time to repair your intuition compass for a while. You *can* get back on track. Maybe reading this book will help just a little with that. That's my hope. And if your intuition compass is already in tip-top shape, you can savor *Red Flags: Tales of Love and Instinct*, recognizing all that you've achieved alongside the authors of these stories and be proud of your sure-footed journey.

DO YOU BELIEVE IN GOD? AND OTHER SECOND-DATE QUESTIONS

ADRIANNE BEER

"I buy all my plants in Ohio."

He hadn't asked. But as he looked around my apartment, I felt embarrassed about the quantity of green. As if plants were a luxury I didn't deserve. "They're really cheap there," I added.

He smiled. His eyes lingered too long at my cork board, at the cut-outs, childhood photos, and a condom wrapper with the Sears Tower on it that read "Chicago Wraps It." I thought it was cool until he saw it. I was intimidated by him, as well as annoyed. He was not handsome, but the way that he sang made me overlook the balding patch of ginger hair he kept covered with greasy ball caps. He was tall. It gave him the ability to look down on me and down my shirt. Which he did while we waited in line for ice cream earlier that evening. I chose a cotton candy-flavored cone while he stared.

"You have good books," he said, pacing slowly through the room.

"Thank you."

I handed him a glass of water.

He laughed. "This is really warm."

"Oh shit. I'm sorry, my water runs hot. I'll get ice. Sorry."

He sat down on my only chair, avoiding the small loveseat where our legs would have grazed. He talked a lot, too much for one person. He's a Catholic but isn't sure about god. He's a bike mechanic. That's how we met. I purchased a kickstand, and he insisted on installing it. He knew the band on my shirt, so I asked him to get coffee with me.

He plays the banjo better than the guitar, and he volunteers at a shelter on Thursdays. He hasn't gotten over his mother's death yet, and two years ago his ex-girlfriend wrote a Tumblr blog about their abusive relationship. I knew most of these things already; I did my due diligence before pursuing him. By that, I mean I Googled his name, and the third link was Paul-ThomasIsMyAbuser.tumblr.com. I read the blog multiple times before our first date. I knew two things: I believed her, and I wanted to be with him. That was problematic, I know.

When he told me about the blog, he watched me closely. I smiled because I felt uncomfortable, and I knew I was going to lie to him by pretending I hadn't read it. I asked him questions: Was it true? What was the worst thing she said about you? Was she hotter than me? I didn't ask the last one but wanted to.

He described their relationship to me. He described how he was manipulative, how maybe he was emotionally abusive, but he never physically or sexually abused her like she claimed. She had posted the Tumblr blog the morning before his Southwest tour. She timed it perfectly so that it would make the most impact. I would have done the same. Months before the Tumblr went live, NPR wrote an article about him, and he had a small international tour booked. He said the backlash from the Tumblr thing manifested in empty venues and Internet friends confronting him with "I read about you." He said he didn't lose anyone close to him, but he did lose musical connections. I laughed at that absurdity.

He told me how he was scared of new relationships, particularly with women. Most recently he had only been sleeping with men. But he missed having sex with women. When he said this, he looked at me in a way that was meant to be charming. All I could think about was if he was a top or a bottom.

I gave him moments of false vulnerability. I gave him bits and pieces of my previous relationships. Particularly the one that ended with an arrested college football player, which left me more bruised than I admitted. I watched as he watched me, waiting for his next turn to speak. In the blog post by his ex-girlfriend, she said he was a narcissist. This was my least favorite thing about him. That, and the way he walked made him look incredibly uncoordinated.

We stayed sitting across from each other until 1:30 in the morning. When he finished his stories, I walked him to his car. We hugged because he pretended to be a good man. When we parted, I stood too close to him and asked if I would see him again.

He said, "Yeah, we should be pals."

Then he walked to his old, gold Camry. When I got back inside and looked in the mirror, I saw a large stain on my shirt from the cotton candy ice cream.

A LESSON IN A MINUTE

BOBBY ROLLINS

Y ou asked to get back together.

We agreed to meet in a diner. You were, just like before, late. When you showed up and sat across from me, my eyes stayed on the wall clock behind you. With its thick frame and black numbers, and its thin stuttering, red second-hand, the clock counted our time together with each fragmented tick.

Fifty-four, fifty-five, fifty-six.

Fifty-seven seconds is enough time for a person to walk a city block, or make a peanut butter and banana sandwich, or say the alphabet three times. It's enough time for the waitress to bring a coffee and menu.

Fifty-seven seconds was also enough time for you to recite a transparently insincere apology, sit back smugly, and assume all was forgiven.

At fifty-eight seconds you became distracted and checked your phone. I saw your dull, self-absorbed eyes mirrored in a scroll of relentless waste on the screen.

At fifty-nine seconds, I rose and left without breaking

stride, fueled by a new appreciation that it was entirely up to me to make sure that every second really does count.

SILENT CHOIR

CLAY HUNT

I stood half naked in my bathroom with a towel shielding the lower half of my body. "You are a champion and a stud," I said. My index fingers pointed at my image in the steamy mirror. "You are going on this date, and it will be the shit!"

It had been a while since I'd dated. I was 25 years old, and I was going out with a 19-year-old woman named Alex. I had met her at a coffee shop a week before. After getting rejected, having many failed dates, and wearing out my thumb swiping on Tinder, I was beginning to think that I was an unwanted pound dog who barked nonsense, had a bad attitude, disgusting, grungy fur, and dingleberries dangling from its butt. The dating scene was rough.

I wanted to take control of myself again. Now that I had scored this date, the dirty dog inside of me morphed into a majestic wolf. I was ready to howl in confidence, rather than wallow in pity. I dropped the towel from my waist and put on what I thought were my best clothes: black skinny jeans, a black Circle Takes the Square shirt, a black denim jacket with assorted band buttons on it, and a black pair of Adidas.

I had gulped three cups of coffee in the last hour. I thought I was thinking clearly, but my mind was flustered. I paced back and forth, repeatedly checking my face for imperfections and washing my hands at least three times. I wanted them to be as clean as possible.

My phone lit up from the other side of the room. I walked over and read, "I'm here."

I scurried to the mirror. "You got this, buddy," I whimpered.

I walked out to my front yard and saw her pickle-green Ford Echo with faded paint on the front end. I smelled tobacco burning as she leaned up against her dinky car. She wore short shorts and a tight green t-shirt. Her short, blonde hair made her chipmunk cheeks glow, and her smile showed big white teeth. I also smiled as I looked at her hazel eyes. She threw her cigarette on the ground, squishing it with her sparkling Vans.

"Hey! It's good to see you again," she said.

She gave me a hug.

"You, too!" I said.

She knew a good neighborhood restaurant to get food. We got in her car, and she drove us to the eatery. On the way, we smoked cigarettes and made first-date small talk: "So what do you do?" "What kind of music do you like?" "Are you in school?"

She told me she was an English major at Cabrillo College, loved to read, and worked at a 24-hour diner on Soquel Avenue. I told her that I also went to Cabrillo, was in a hip-hop group, and worked at Foster's Freeze. She seemed impressed.

My pep-talk in front of the mirror at home echoed in my head: *Man, she's hot. I hope I can keep it together. Everything will be fine.*

We arrived at the restaurant and sat at a small table across from each other. The place had bright walls and flimsy tables and chairs. There wasn't much space and I kept tapping my fingers on my upper thigh, trying to concentrate.

You're doing good. She is still smiling.

Within the first few bites of my dinner, out of nowhere, chemical warfare commenced. Maybe it was nerves, or all that coffee, or whatever...I felt pressure moving through my intestines. I let out a couple of quiet but noticeable notes from the tuba.

The last one wasn't a note at all, but a silent choir of shit.

If she only knew what she had gotten herself into. I was an adult who shit his pants. I had other qualities that might have flagged her attention, but I knew then that I fucked up, and that I probably was no good for her. *At least this will save the embarrassment of her getting to know my shitty side.* I knew I had to get up and go to the bathroom. I knew this would raise suspicion, but I had to. Things weren't going well, and I was to blame.

She was in the middle of a sentence about her dad, something about him also being in recovery, but I couldn't wait any longer.

"Hey," I announced. "I'm going to use the bathroom."

Her eyes squinted and her posture straightened.

I was already halfway down the cramped hallway before Alex could reply. I slammed the door. My hands shook like a drummer playing a blast beat as I dropped my pants and boxers to the ground then kicked them to the wall. I saw my boxers caked in nose-punishing poop and my butt was an aftermath of an explosion. I hobbled over to the toilet and used two full rolls of toilet paper in an attempt to clean up. I used the sink to rinse myself. In the midst of these manic movements, I locked eyes with my old friend in the mirror. He was just some faceless soldier, losing a war with himself.

Napoleon Bonaparte was no stranger to war. He was as

confident as he was short, although researchers say he was about 5'6". He conquered and controlled Spain, Belgium, and the Netherlands. He also wrote a romance novel about a soldier in a doomed relationship titled, *Clisson et Eugénie*. He was a sentimental man, as well as a ruthless colonizer, but he also had a good sense of hygiene.

Napoleon traveled with a silver bidet. A bidet is a hygienic device with origins in France. It is used to wash one's genitals and anus after taking a shit. You squat down, twist the knob, and water shoots up your butt. It's quite sanitary, but they are not commonly used in the U.S.A. (and we say we are the best country in the world). I assume he had a way of connecting to some kind of plumbing wherever he went. The silver acted as a defense against germs and kept the device sterile. Napoleon loved his bidet so much that, in his will, he gave it to his son.

The confidence and hygiene this man possessed were superb, yet I currently had neither. I desperately wished for a bidet in that room. My romantic reign on this date was about to end, and a bidet could have been my secret weapon to win it back.

I scrutinized my reflection and asked, *Jesus fucking Christ. What are you doing?*

There I was, that unwanted dog, as I separated my shit-filled underwear from my pants and bundled my boxers in the plastic bag that lined the trash. The ripe smell caused me to gag, and I had to hold back from vomiting.

I cleaned up the brown mess the best I could, but there was one glop of slushy poop on my jeans. Luckily, I had chosen to wear black. I washed my hands like it was with holy water. I looked into the mirror one more time. *Good luck, asshole.* I trudged back to the table.

"Hey, I'm ready to go," I said.

"Oh," Alex said as her lips puffed out, "I wanted to---"

"I'd really like to go," I said.

My face clenched and forced a courteous smile.

"Ummm, okay," she said.

Her eyes scanned the table, then looked at me. Her smile was absent. We paid. I took giant steps towards the exit door, and she followed. *Can she smell that?*

At least I didn't have hemorrhoids. Napoleon suffered them often. That is why he carried a bidet. Some scholars say it was because he spent so much time on his horse. The irritating veins must have poked at his brain like a mischievous kid poking a dead dog. Maybe that is why he was so angry. Who knows? What I did know was that this embarrassment poked at my brain. Hemorrhoids would be a better excuse. Napoleon managed, though, and he was able to get what he wanted. I wasn't so confident.

I must have looked like I had a prosthetic leg by the way I walked towards the car. My head faced the ground.

"Hey!" Alex demanded.

My face was red, and my eyes were watery.

"What happened? Why do you look so tense? Were you crying? What's wrong?"

"I shit my pants," I said.

"ARE YOU SERIOUS?" she asked.

Her smile returned. The roar of her laughter echoed as she locked arms with me.

"Yeah." I forced a smile.

She looked up at me with her merciful, beautiful smile. I could feel her laughter while her chest was pressed against mine. And then she kissed me.

"Wanna go back to your place?"

My head titled to the left.

"S-sure," I uttered.

I had conquered the night! Well, I surrendered. I wonder if

Napoleon ever had an accident like this or misplaced his precious bidet. I wonder if he ever had to settle for a lesser bidet, one that wasn't made of silver. I would have settled for a plastic bidet at that moment, but I learned that a sink works just as well if that is all you have. I realized that I was human that night, and that Alex was a human capable of humor, forgiveness, smiles, and compassion. We ended up dating for a couple months, and poo wasn't the reason we broke up. Sometimes shit just happens. But humility can stretch out and absorb messes like sheets of tissue, and sometimes you can wipe the fear away with squares of truth.

HALLOWEEN HORROR-ISH NIGHT

CHRISTOPHER GAUNTT

I n recollecting my worst dating moments, three come to mind. The second worst is of a woman who was delusional to such an extent that she believed Jesus was sleeping on her couch, that we were destined to be married, and that I wanted her to kill me for some reason I couldn't quite fathom. Fortunately, this all happened in our initial flirtation stage, and I had enough sense to escape any further entanglements.

The worst was a woman who trapped me in an 18-hour argument over the meaning of "have a good time:" She thought I meant casual sex; I was thinking more along the lines of going bowling. She blocked me from leaving her apartment multiple times when I tried to leave. There is *much* more to it than that, but you will have to forgive me for not regaling you further with this particular tale of horror—it is just too traumatic to relive in the telling.

So that leaves me with the third worst. A story that is not nearly as terrifying, and although no joy to experience, is quite amusing nevertheless in the retelling. This story begins with a date and ends with a date.

A friend of mine, Jill, thought this woman, Sharon, and I would make a good match. The pitch was good, and we agreed to go on a date.

It was a sunny Saturday morning in mid-October when I picked her up at her Los Angeles apartment building, which also happened to be where our matchmaker friend Jill lived. Sharon and I had a light lunch and then went for a hike in a popular spot in the canyons.

[A pause to kill an ant crawling across my desk. It's summer, it's hot, and the ants are invading my space. They are crawling out of the walls onto the cables that lead to my computer and my desk. It's very distracting—especially when they crawl across my monitor. It's not a typo, it's an ant. Sigh.]

The hike was lovely: witty conversation, dodging rattle snakes, holding hands. You know, the usual sort of thing that happens on hiking dates. Afterwards we stopped at a little store for hydration and snacks before heading back to her place.

At the store we ran into a pair of her friends. They were a really nice gay couple, Tim and Zach, who were super excited about their upcoming Halloween party. Apparently, it was an annual event that they really put their hearts and souls into. Tim talked about how they went all out with the decorations and that it was going to be super scary. Zach said the food was going to be choice. Then they invited us to come to the party.

I happen to be *really* into getting dressed up for masquerade balls, themed parties, and Halloween in particular. So, I was all-in when they invited us to come. I turned to Sharon and asked her how she would feel about a second date. She said, "Sounds like it will be fun" or something of the like. I don't recall at the time if I noticed whether she was genuinely interested. Perhaps she was, perhaps she wasn't. Anyway, the only signal flag color I saw at the time was green. Before we parted ways, Tim made it a particular point to say that we had to dress scary; "Otherwise, you won't even be allowed in." Heck, yeah! I was pumped.

A few days later, Sharon and I talked on the phone to make arrangements. She informed me that a couple of her friends, Jack and Cynthia, were invited as well, so she asked if it would be cool if we went on a double date.

"The more the merrier," I said, and I meant it.

So, the plan was that I was going to go to her apartment, then Jack and Cynthia would pick us up to carpool to the party.

It's now maybe a week later on the day of the party. Before then, Sharon and I had talked a few times on the phone to go over plans, what we were going to wear, general chit chat. Nothing that raised any warning flags. Did I mention I really get into dressing up in costume? (I just checked, and yes, I apparently already mentioned it. Okay, good. Wanted to be sure.) Well, I'd had this Halloween costume idea simmering for many years: a dead jester. And this seemed to be the perfect scary event to try it out.

The costume was cobbled together from several different outfits. The base was a skeleton shirt composed of pitch-black cloth with white 3D foam bones, a ribcage and arms, sewn into it. Layered over that was an Elizabethan white shirt that was shredded, and blood stained. The shredding revealed the bones beneath. Over that was a slightly tattered, black-velvet doublet with droopy sleeves. For pants, I wore a pair of black-and-white, diamond-patterned pantaloons that tied off at the knee with blood-red ribbons that shook with little bells on the ends. Below, I wore bone-white hose stockings with some floppy, black Renaissance-ish boots. On my head, I had a custom-made, three-point jester hat that was black and white with skulls and crossbones sewn in. Naturally, it was stuffed so the points stuck out. At the end of each point, there were additional bells shaped like skulls. A foam skull prosthetic was glued to my face with spirit gum. For good measure, I added some rotting flesh and maggots coming out of my neck. A decaying motif on my face was created out of white, brown, and green makeup. For accessories, I wore very realistic-looking skeleton gloves, and a leather belt with a leather pouch to carry my wallet, ID, keys, etc. The final touch was a black rod with a tiny skull and some ratty strips of blood-stained linen attached to the end. It was, if I may say, fucking awesome.

It was also a real pain to assemble and wear. The bone mask and makeup pulled at my face, which became more uncomfortable the longer I wore it. The jester hat was heavy and had to be tied on pretty tight, so it didn't fall off. Because my costume was so complicated, I wasn't sure how long it would take for me to get ready. So, I started fairly early in the afternoon, thinking it would take several hours because I had to do everything myself. I very much overestimated how long it would take. Thus, I found myself all set and ready to go around 4 PM.

[Die, ant! Die! You insectoid invader!]

If I recall correctly, we were supposed to meet up with Jack and Cynthia around 7 PM so that we could arrive at the party around 8 PM. Well, I didn't want to just sit in my apartment the whole time. So, I called Sharon to check in: I was ready earlier than expected and could come over at any time.

Orange flag: She said, "Jack and Cynthia haven't arrived yet. I'll call you when they get here."

I asked, "So, I should just wait here until you call?"

"Yes. I'll call when you can come over."

That seemed odd to me. If the situation had been reversed, I would have invited her to come over. Maybe not right away, but I would have said something like, "Why don't you come around 6 PM?" But there was no such invitation.

"Okay," I replied.

"Okay," she said. "I'll call you later."

Click.

Well, I guess technically it was just the silence of a dropped call, since there really aren't any "clicks" at the end of a cell phone conversation.

So, I sat there, in full costume, waiting. I was already getting a slight headache from wearing the hat because it was tied on so tight, but since it was such a pain to attach, I left it on. Also, my ankle started acting up a little.

Regarding my ankle, as this will be relevant later: I am a social dancer. A few nights before, I went out dancing with some friends and had a very rare moment when I managed to step in just the wrong way to give myself a sprain. Nothing I couldn't walk on as long as I was careful, but the doctor had prescribed some mild pain killers to help reduce the discomfort. Anyway, I took some meds then so that I wouldn't need them later.

Five o'clock came and went. Followed by six o'clock, then seven, eight...

At this point, the warning flag had gone from orange to red. We should have been at the party by then.

...nine...

I should have ended it right there, but I was dealing with the sunken-cost fallacy. If you've never heard of it, it's an important concept. Look it up. I can't possibly describe it with any justice.

Ten PM rolled around. I had been sitting in my apartment in full costume for six hours. I had a headache, and my ankle was getting achy, too. I was ready to call it a night and was just about to remove the hat when the phone rang. It was Sharon.

Jack and Cynthia had finally arrived at her apartment, so I could "come over now." It took me half an hour to get there.

Jack and Cynthia were dressed as Gomez and Morticia Adams. A classic choice. They were very nice. I had met them before at other events as they were also friends with Jill, our common acquaintance. Sharon was dressed as a sexy devil. It was accurate, in hindsight, on several levels.

My date was kind of quiet and wasn't really interacting with me very much. She answered my questions in very short sentences and never bothered to ask me any questions in return. That was easily a yellow flag, but I was too preoccupied with the discomfort of the mask pulling at my face and the headache from the jester hat. So, I gave up trying to engage with her and switched over to conversing with Jack and Cynthia.

It was another half an hour or so before we finally arrived at the party, around 11 PM-ish. I was then going on seven hours in a costume that had become increasingly uncomfortable. The headache was getting worse, and my ankle was really starting to act up since the meds had worn off. Unfortunately, the one thing I forgot to put in my pouch was the pain killers. This was both a bad and good thing.

Anyway, as we got closer to our destination, my mood began to improve, and my aches subsided in a burst of adrenaline. Finally! Super scary party! Good times ahead!

[Another ant. It must be killed...Mission accomplished.]

We found a place to park that wasn't too far of a walk. I favored my foot a little bit, but not so much as to give away that I had an injury—'cause, ya know, male ego wanting to tough it out and not draw attention to it. When we got within eyesight of the address, the door opened and out came a large, bearded man, wearing a pink ballet leotard and white tutu, and probably ballet slippers. He lit up a cigarette as he left. At first, I was thinking, "I hope that's not the party we are going to..." As we got closer, I realized it was. But then I thought, *Well, maybe he got turned away because he wasn't dressed scary*. Although, I guess in some ways he was dressed scary, but not in the way the hosts implied when they pitched the party to us at the little store. Nonetheless, a yellow flag was raised.

There were cobwebs and plastic spiders on the bushes and railings leading up to the door. *That's a good start,* I thought. We rang the doorbell, which gave a hokey "muahahahha" ring. At least it was in the spirit of the evening. The door opened, and we were greeted by Zach, one of the hosts, dressed in his scariest costume, a large-sized container full of McDonald's ® French Fries ™. Now, I will grant you that the calories and nutritional value of McDonald's French Fries are a scary thing. I personally can't eat the stuff without my stomach getting a case of the runs. However, I began to suspect that Zach and Tim's definition of scary was very different from mine. The flag was upgraded from yellow to orange.

I smiled (not that you could necessarily tell through my mask) and said hello, along with the others. Zach was super happy to see us, so he let us in. There was almost no one there. The decorations were, well, not at all scary. They were poorly done, very kitschy, and looked like most of the decorations had been picked up last minute at a 99-cent store. Normally, I wouldn't care about this sort of thing–if I hadn't been in an actual scary costume–which they *insisted* was necessary to get in–for nearly seven hours by that point.

Well, I guess it can't get much worse, I thought.

Tim came up to join Zach. "So happy you could make it. Wow! Your dead jester costume is amazing!"

"Thank you," I replied.

Tim turned to Sharon. "So, is this your date?"

Sharon's reply: "Oh no, he's just a friend."

?

Flag went from orange, bypassed regular red, and went on to pirates-are-going-to-capture-you-and-kill-you-no-quarter-given blood red.

This was the first time I was told we were not on a date. Had I been paying attention to all the warning signal flags, I might have suspected something had changed since we last agreed that we were going on a date. Though it would have been nice to have been informed of the status change before I started getting into costume some nine hours earlier.

I should mention that the few people already at the party were all staring at us new folks, especially at the cool-looking scary dead jester. The apartment was not very large, nor was the music very loud, so there is no possible way that they could have missed the announcement by the sexy devil lady that the cool scary jester was just-a-friend-not-a-date. And, as it turns out, the majority of the remaining guests were the hosts' gay male friends. So, it wasn't long before several guys were chatting me up. Sharon, bless her heart, immediately sidestepped out of their way, and booked it for the kitchen where the alcohol was, abandoning me to unwanted attention.

I politely interacted with the fellas. They were all nice enough. But when it was clear they weren't getting anywhere with me, they eventually wandered off.

[Quick break to get a snack, only to find my refrigerator SWARMING with ants. Hundreds and hundreds of them, inside and out: both the refrigerator and even the freezer where their cold dead carcasses line the inside of the door. Exterminator has been called. Waiting to hear back.]

Being relieved of the other partiers' attention for the time being, I decided to find the three members of the group I came in with. I found them on the balcony. They had come to the same conclusion that this party sucked and none of us wanted to be there. That was a relief, because I couldn't wait to leave, which is highly unusual for someone like me. The problem was we hadn't been there for more than ten, twenty minutes at most. The other three people knew the hosts personally, and so none of them wanted to say we were bailing.

By this time, my foot was aching something terrible, I had a major headache, and I just didn't give a shit anymore—so, I stepped up with "I'll do it."

I went over to the talking French Fries and begged their pardon by telling the truth: "I am so sorry, but I have a major headache, I injured my foot, the meds have worn off, and unfortunately I left them at home. And since they're my ride, I need them to take me home. Thanks for the invite, and I wish I could have stuck around." Well, I guess that last bit wasn't all that truthful.

Now you would think most hosts would just let it go at that regardless of what they think the truth might be. I expected something along the lines of: "Oh, okay. I'm sorry to hear that. I understand. Thank you so much for coming and maybe you can make it next year. Safe travels and I hope you feel better!" You know, polite normal conversation. Instead, I get from Mr. French Fries: "Oh really? Is THAT the reason why you are leaving? Because of your FOOT? It's not because the party SUCKS?"

Wow. I was floored. Did he overhear our conversation on the balcony? I don't think I've ever been met with actual hostility when leaving a party before. You know what? Didn't matter. Because the truth was still: "Yeah, actually, it really is my foot. I really do have a major headache. And I really did forget my meds. So, I'm leaving."

And I left. I don't remember what the other couple or my date-not-really-a-date said, and I didn't care. I just limped back towards the car and took off my jester hat, which I had been wearing for who knows how many hours by that point.

When we got to the car, I just wanted to go home. But the others were hungry and wanted to eat something before going back to Sharon's apartment building. We settled on a deli. As we were driving over there, I started removing the bone face mask and other prosthetics. And yet, as though I hadn't been through enough, the others in the car were saying, "No! Don't take it off! You'll look so cool! The folks at the deli need to see this!"

"No, they don't. I've been wearing this thing for over eight hours now, and I just can't wear it anymore. It's pulling my face off, and it's extremely uncomfortable. I'm not going to eat like this." There was more pushback, but eventually they relented. By the time we got to the deli, I was finally a little better. My face was feeling less undead, and my headache was starting to fade. We sat at a booth with Jack and Cynthia on one side, and me and Sharon on the other.

[Ant invasion update: I'm still waiting for the extermination people to call me back. But I have sprayed the refrigerator and freezer with ant killing bug spray in the meantime. There are hundreds and hundreds of ant bodies writhing in globules of insecticide. Their cries of pain and agony, if I could hear them, would be falling on unsympathetic ears.]

So...now we're eating and talking about various things. My date-not-really-a-date decides to tell this story about how she went onto the Internet and took an IQ test. How'd it go? She was still a genius.

Still?

Apparently, this is something that she does on a regular basis. She goes online and takes an IQ test to make sure she still qualifies as a genius.

Hm.

And then one of the pair across from us, I think it was Cynthia, said that she had read an article that stated people who were geniuses sometimes have trouble with social interactions. My response was something along the lines of: "Oh yes, one of my friends is a genius and he's absolutely socially inept."

SMACK!

It happened so fast that I didn't see it coming.

My date-definitely-not-a-date-anymore hit me in the face with the flat side of the menu, hard. My face was already hurting and sensitive from pulling the prosthetics off earlier, so having the menu smashed in my face stung a lot more than it might have otherwise.

"Well," I declared to the group, "I guess that's it for my part of the conversation for the rest of the evening." And other than placing my order, I spoke no more.

My guess is that Sharon took what I said as an intentional, direct insult. And maybe it was. I was rather fed up with the whole situation. It's too bad she didn't wait a few more seconds to hear the rest of what I was going to say, which was that I have a high IQ and can be socially awkward at times. Nonetheless, on reflection, it seems to me that smacking somebody in the face with a menu rather than debating a point, saying that somebody who was actually your date is not actually your date, and not just being upfront and letting somebody know that you don't actually want to go on a date with them, and let them stew in a costume for five hours before inviting them over, kinda seems like social ineptness to me. As far as I was concerned, Cynthia's point was totally validated in that moment.

Anyway, the conversation went on to other things I took no interest in because I had no desire to interact with anybody at the table. The food came. I ate it. They talked about more things. We finished the food, paid for it, and we all got into the car and left. It took another half an hour to get back to Sharon's apartment building.

It is now probably 1:00 AM, and I've been in this fucking costume for nine hours. Even though I am clearly no longer under any obligation to do "date-ish" stuff, I was raised to be a courteous person. When you are on a date, you escort them to and from the door out of politeness and for safety reasons. That's what you do. And normally it's never been an issue, even if the date didn't go well. But in this instance, as we were pulling up to the front of the apartment building, I found myself thinking, *Shit, I have to escort her to her door. I don't want to walk her back to her apartment. I just want to go home. But it would be rude of me not to.* Etc.

I decided to just suck it up and offer to escort her. But before I could say anything, Sharon announced, "Oh, you don't have to escort me to my door. I'm going home with Cynthia and Jack." This took me by surprise. And if the reaction of Jack's face that I spotted in the rearview mirror and Cynthia's body language was any indication, they were taken by surprise as well. I took the gift, got out of their car, said my goodbyes, and limped over to my car. But I couldn't help thinking to myself, *I bet they're just going to drive around the block and then drop her off.* And I was good with that. I went home, took my meds, took off my costume, took a long shower, and went to bed. The next day I got a phone call from Jill, the now no-longer-reliable matchmaker.

"Hi, Jill."

"Hey. So, what happened last night?" There was something in her tone that made me think she already knew the answer to that question. I related the tale anyway—all of it, in extreme detail. More so than what I have abbreviated in this printed telling.

There was a pause as she processed this information, and then she declared, "Hmm, I think I believe *you*."

"Huh? What did Sharon tell you?"

"She told me a different story."

"How different?"

"Completely different."

"Care to share?"

"She said that you went to a pub, had dinner, played some pool, and when you escorted her back to her door, you tried to kiss her, but she wouldn't let you."

I was speechless for a few seconds, absorbing the information.

"Are you fucking kidding me?" I wasn't angry; I was just in a state of shock and surprise. I mean, it wasn't even remotely close to the truth.

I said, "Well, Jack and Cynthia were there, so you can check with them."

"Oh, I will. And I'm sorry I introduced you two. I really thought you would hit it off."

"Well, I certainly got hit."

Okay, I probably did not say that last line, but it would have been perfectly on point.

We probably talked about other things, but I was too preoccupied to participate fully in the conversation. I was still stunned that Sharon had totally lied about what happened on the date.

Jill and I rang off and that was that.

Or so I thought.

About two weeks later I found a voicemail waiting for me when I got into the office. It was from Sharon. In the voicemail, she actually admitted to not going home with Jack and Cynthia, that they just drove around the block and let her off at her apartment. And then she asked that I call her some time.

I hit the delete button.

[The exterminators are coming on Friday. I have to move furniture away from the walls wherever ants might be coming in. All my food either needs to be thrown out or wrapped in plastic. And then I have to vacate the premises for four to five hours. If only I could destroy them all with a delete button.]

BETTER LUCK NEXT TIME

NAZIA KAMALI

O ne of my sister's colleagues had a very attractive profile picture on Facebook. Impressed by his chiseled features and dark-brown eyes, I sent him a friend request. This introduction led to frequent chats on Messenger, and soon we hopped onto Whatsapp and calls. However, by the time we became good friends, he had moved to Dubai, and I left Dehradun, our hometown in India, to pursue higher education in Ropar.

While I was in Ropar, he came home twice, but we weren't able to see each other. Every time he was in India, we repeated the same sentences: "I wish we could meet...I wish I could take out some time from my schedule to see you...I wish we were in the same city..."

Five long years later, when I came home after submitting my dissertation, we were in Dehradun at the same time. My anticipation had been whipped into a frenzy by then. I vividly remember that it was a slightly chilly morning on November the 17th. I was standing in the yard looking at the sun-bathed, clear blue sky when my phone pinged.

"Reached home last night..." His four-word message made my heart jump with joy.

My hands automatically dialed his number.

"Helllloooooo," he replied playfully.

"Let's meet up." The urgency in my tone seemed to stun him. He zoned out for a second or two. I repeated my words.

"When?"

"Tomorrow..."

"Why not this evening?" *That was fast,* I thought and smiled.

In that moment, I could scarcely predict that the date would leave me flustered and confused. He reached the coffee shop a full thirty-five minutes late. I sat there like a fool, waiting for him. For a punctual person like me that was the first warning sign. *Was he not excited to finally see me? Why did he suggest meeting that evening if he was busy?*

When I was just about to leave, he walked through the door, smiled at me, and apologized, mumbling some lame excuse about all the traffic lights on the way turning red exactly when he was about to cross.

I looked at him with fuming eyes, but damn...he was hot! Tall and broad-shouldered, like one of those models in the cologne advertisements. A navy-blue sweater hugged his well-sculpted body. The warm smile that played on his lips calmed me. He sat down, and we began talking.

"How is the weather?" I asked, regretting it the next instant.

"Cool, cold, I mean hot...You are asking about Dubai, right? Dubai is hot. Dehradun is cold."

"Aah..."

And then, as if to salvage the situation, he began rambling not-so-funny one-liners.

"What do you call a fish without an eye? A fsh... Do you know what to do with Velcro? Rip it off..."

I knew that he wasn't very good with words, but I had no idea he was *that* poor at telling jokes face-to-face. Every time he cracked a joke, it took me several beats to realize that I need to fake a laugh.

Why did he feel compelled to crack such poor jokes, or "PJ's" as we call them in India, when he had no skill? I had known him for five years, and he had never tried to be so silly over chats and phone calls.

Maybe he is nervous.

Soon the conversation steered into other directions. He told me about his bid for a new project, so I inquired about the company he was working for these days.

"MAC"

"Wow, you are working for the operating system of Apple?"

"It's a makeup brand."

"MAC is a brand of makeup?"

"You didn't know?"

Holy shit, this man knows more about makeup than I do.

Things became weirder after that. I have always been fascinated with gadgets and their specifications. Recalling my classes in engineering college, I explained how a Printed Circuit Board of a CPU motherboard is designed. In reply, he boasted that he knew how it was done. He had learned it online.

Why would a person in marketing learn that? I don't need him to know everything that I know. A man with complexes; why hadn't realized this before? Calm down, maybe we both are just not settled in yet, I kept telling myself. I shouldn't judge someone that easily. It's a bad habit. We have been friends for such a long time. Give him a little more credit.

After about an hour, I said, "Why don't we order something? We have been sitting here for some time now."

"Oh, yeah, I kind of forgot."

In my excitement to meet him, I had skipped lunch. Waiting for him at an empty table made me hungrier. This thoughtlessness got on my nerves. *Who forgets to order something for a girl who crossed half the town and five years just to meet him?*

I wish it was the last stupid thing he did that evening.

When we finally got up to leave, he walked in front of me, reached for the glass door, opened it, and closed it behind him. He literally closed the door in my face. And when I stepped out of the cafe, face burning with anger and embarrassment, he looked at me sheepishly and said, "Oh, you were there, too."

I'd had numerous encounters with men before, but this one was breath-takingly bad. And, after all those years, it was truly a shock. I felt myself float above my body.

He offered to drop me home, but why would I take this moron home?

When I told my sister about her ex-colleague, she couldn't stop laughing.

"I didn't know he was that stupid," she said. "Better luck next time," she added mischievously.

THE TINY GENERAL

LISA MONTAGNE

S anger, California, is a Central Valley farming community surrounded by huge swaths of grape vines. Instead of wine grapes, these vineyards cure raisins that lounge like tiny sunbathers in the hot, dry sun. Until I was five years old, we lived in a rented house there. My strong, handsome father was the agriculture teacher and the Future Farmers of America (F.F.A.) leader at the high school. My mother, who had been a Houston, Texas, socialite, was suffocating under the weight of a po-dunk town in the middle of no-where. Even though my mother wasn't exactly happy, she was a good mother, and she took me to swimming lessons to combat the summer heat.

She dropped me off at the public pool in our blue, four-door Chevy, which was big enough to sail on the high seas. I wore my pink bathing suit, a god-awful bathing cap bedecked with rubber daisies, and tiny rubber flip-flops. Draped around my neck, I had a yellow smiley-face beach towel twice my size. While holding on to the edge of the pool, I dunked my head under water and blew bubbles, kicking my little legs like crazy.

Only weeks before, putting my head under was terrifying, but that day, I mastered it. At the end of the lesson, I slid into my flip-flops and flourished the towel around me like a superhero's cape. I was giddy with my new superpower, and like a little Napoleon, I stood on the steps of the pool house in triumph, hands on hips, waiting for my mother to pick me up. And I waited...

I loved my mother dearly. I lost her way too young. She possessed the most raw, quick intelligence of any person I've ever met. But, god love her, she had almost no common sense whatsoever. She could tell amusing stories and sing funny songs, make up rhymes about lunch on the spot, and zing one-liners with comedic timing. She got the highest score on the Scrabble board of anyone ever. She could tell me the most obscure trivia. I used to test her on the spot: Who was the attorney general in 1923? She knew that. 1823? That, too. She could remember any phone number she ever knew. She sang all the planets in order of placement from the sun. She could play the piano like an angel. She walked around the house in her underwear singing and playing the ukulele. She had even been a college beauty queen. Everyone adored her. Think of a less flimsy Elizabeth Taylor.

But when it came down to it, my father would have preferred a more practical wife. Having been raised by maids, my mother couldn't clean the house worth doody. She couldn't manage the household budget or her diet. She would never, ever get off the phone. Seemingly unaware that children need regular sleep, she expected me to stay up all night playing music with her. And she could not, if her life depended on it, be on time.

Even at four years old, I knew that she was struggling. My child's heart pumped with empathy for her. But I was too young to be anything but irritated. Even then, I valued punctuality. *Where was she?* It was hot. I was thirsty. Soon I would have to tinkle. The rubber cap squeezed my head. My bathing suit was almost dry, for crying out loud. Most importantly, I was ready to announce my victory that day in the pool. I could blow bubbles with my head under water, but where the heck was my mother?

Right, I concluded. *I might as well walk.*

After my triumph in the pool, my confidence tank was spilling over with white-hot fuel. Alerting nearby adults never occurred to me. My instinct was to rely on myself. It was more than a mile to get home, but I knew exactly where to go. Still uncorrupted by the warfare of life, I was a fresh, patriotic recruit with an internal navigation system that rivaled the most accomplished sea captain.

With my towel now draped like a French soldier's sash, I looked right and then left at the crosswalk to check for cars. I stepped into the street down off the enormous, grey cement curb. A trickle of sprinkler run-off spread like a river across the roadway, seducing me like the sirens of the sea. I made it across the street. This was a day of firsts, and my mother was nowhere to be seen.

I was spurred by annoyance—both at my mother and at having been slighted so frivolously by the fates. I deserved a victory parade. So, I gave myself one. Holding my head high, I strutted down the sidewalk past the middle school where the big kids lurked, and past houses on street corners where I never been allowed before. Finally, I turned the corner by the school-yard where a bee had stung me on the knee a few weeks earlier. *Take that, bee,* I thought, with bravado. *Try and get me now.*

I was almost home—just one more street to cross. Again, I checked right and left for cars. I adjusted my towel, tugged at the rubber cap, and stepped out into the street. A few more steps would land me in the safe harbor of my yard. All I could think of was being thirsty and having to tinkle at the same time. I wanted a glass of water while I was on the toilet. But would my mother be there to get me a glass of water? To help me with my bathing suit? Did it matter?

No, she was not there. The front door was locked. Locked! I started to feel more panicked than annoyed. I had marched all that way, and still no mommy. No brother, no father. No one.

Post battle, my mood deflated. A sense of hopelessness crept back, like when they wouldn't let me into Mother's room after her operation. I had stood at her bedroom door, looking through the crack for hours, for days, for they—the united front —my grandparents, my father, my brother—would not let me past the barrier. Now, I had walked home because my mother was late, and I could blow bubbles under water, but I was alone. I sat with a thump on the front stoop, wrapping the towel around me like camouflage.

Finally, I heard a horn and a grinding on the driveway. It was my mother. She flew out of the car on her high heels, flustered and flushed.

"Where were you?!" She picked me up and hugged me to her. "I was so worried! I drove all over looking for you. Why didn't you wait for me? Something could have happened to you! You could have been run over by a car. What happened?!"

"I walked," I said, defiantly, chin up.

"You walked?"

I nodded my head vigorously, the plastic daisies flapping with the motion.

"Lisa Lorraine, how could you?" was all that she said, including my middle name for emphasis.

Later, when she told my father about my campaign,

trooping home alone from the public pool, he was all smiles and very proud.

"She gets her grit from my mother—tough, stubborn, little thing" was all that he said. He'd hoped for a boy, but got me instead, a brave, tiny general, ready to conquer the world.

LOST IN TUNIS

REUBEN TIHI HAYSLETT

I boarded a 15-hour flight from Los Angeles to Tunisia with a pit stop in Istanbul. I'd never even left the country before, much less know any Arabic or French. It'll be fine, I told myself. I read through all the safety precautions outlined by the human rights conference I was attending. Just having a human rights conference in Tunisia was an open target for terrorism, so the conference guide told us to wear muted colored clothes with no brand insignias or slogans, don't bring expensive jewelry, or take anything expensive for that matter. I left my laptop at home.

Part of me secretly hoped I could blend in. Growing up mixed-race in Iowa, nobody was ever sure where I was from at first glance. I have paper-bag brown skin, which would lead most people down the Afro or Latino route (both of which are correct), but then there's the thick, course black beard that no force on this planet seems to be able to tame. And the black hair on my head is curly, but not tightly curled. And then there's my nose. If any feature was my passport to blending in in the

Mediterranean, it would be my prominent nose that tucks in under a pronounced brow ridge.

I figured I could swim in and out of crowds on the streets of Tunis, feeling for the first time in my life what it must be like to not be stared down, to not see strangers' wrinkled foreheads silently telegraphing "What kind of ethnic is that?" I was wrong.

Tunisians are famously slender people, so my beer-belly presence called attention. Once or twice, though, before I opened my mouth and removed all doubt that I was anything but American—except for one gracious elderly woman who said, "No Trump, you Canada"—people would guess, and it was always the same guess.

"Paki?"

"No."

"Oh! American!"

Even Pakistani people I met in Istanbul thought I was Pakistani until I started talking.

To see the "real" Tunis, I skipped out of the conference early, emptied out my pockets, walked through the airport-style metal detector, and flashed my passport to the Armani-suited private security guards with those coiled, plastic earphones draped behind their ears. They held one or more semi-automatic firearms. And like any American idiot, I was magnetically drawn to the medina.

In some ways, Tunis looked like every other large metropolitan city. There are large thoroughfares with sidewalk bistro restaurants, wheat-pasted movie posters about the next new film coming to theaters, and a pleasantly surprising amount of ACAB graffiti. But the North Africa-Middle Eastern stereotype of what most people think the city looks like is the medina. It's packed so closely with buildings, shops, and open-air markets that once you're inside it, it's actually quite dark. The streets can get so narrow that not even bicycles can get through in some parts. And these roads twist so fluidly that when I looked back, I couldn't find the entrance where I came in. In just under five minutes, alone on the other side of the world—and not having the sense to tell anyone where I was going—I was lost.

But I didn't want to look lost. I kept pace with the foot traffic around me and just kept walking. At different forks and intersections, I shrugged and thought, "I can't get more lost," and chose a turn at random. After a few more blocks, the medina opened up. Sunlight streamed into a busy plaza, at the center of which was a mosque.

I took a couple of pictures then an old man tugged at my shirt. When I turned around the man touched my belly (a common reaction I kept getting as a "fat American") and said, "Paki?"

"No," I answered.

"American!"

The old man grabbed my hand, nodded his head toward a street on the left, and we took off running. For the first few streets we bent around at breakneck speed, there were people. Other shoppers, open stores. But then that stopped. The "street" narrowed more, and the buildings got taller, casting more shadows into wherever it was that we were.

My first thought was that this old man was surprisingly fast for his age. My second thought was that I had no idea where I was being taken, or how to get back to the conference. I hoped I had enough charge in my cell phone—in case I needed it for an emergency—and eventually just gave up. In Istanbul, I was similarly stupid and trusting of strangers. I smoked joints on a rooftop terrace with a bunch of hetero Russian guys and one Algerian girl after the bars closed. And then, on my walk home to my hotel, invited an Indian man back to my room. He declined. The worst thing that happened to me in Istanbul was getting caught up buying a rug from one of the most attractive men I've ever seen. So, I figured Tunis couldn't be very much more or less dangerous.

I tried to register anything that could be landmarks to help me figure out how to retrace our steps, but we were moving fast through a section of the medina that had no open stores. No business signs, no street names.

Eventually we ended at the entrance to a furniture store. It didn't look any different from any furniture store I'd seen in America. Very anticlimactic for all this old man's running and urgency.

The old man saw I was disappointed and said, "No, no, no!" and made that universal head cock that means "follow me." We went up a flight of stairs where young men are taking naps on thick rugs inside curved nooks in the wall, and down a hallway to a large room, which is where I found out this old man knows more English than he let on.

"This is Sultan harem bed," he said. "In old times, mosque was palace and here was harem. For Sultan."

The harem bed was half the size of the room, which itself was twice the size of my Long Beach apartment. And the bed frame was solid gold. About six people could fit in that bed at the same time before you could feel crowded. The old man motioned for me to get in.

"In! I take picture for you."

I'd never seen an ancient antiquity outside of a museum before, so I politely declined. But I still snapped pictures, smoothed my hand over one of the gold bedposts. I had never been so close to something so ancient or expensive ever in my life. It was hard to take my eyes off the harem bed.

The man took my hand again, and we left and went up more stairs until we got to the roof. The sun blasted my eyes as he opened the heavy metal door to a sprawling rooftop with worn mosaic archways and benches and now-empty recesses for tiny ponds and fountains. It was so beautiful that I took me a while to look out and see the city. The mosque's minaret loomed in the sky, over the shadowy medina that looked like an urban canyon.

After I snapped photos, the old man guided me to the far end of the rooftop terrace to an altar with a glass bowl and folded paper cards that said "tips" in different languages. I threw in some Tunisian dinar and the old man said, "Ready?" I had no idea what more there was to show me, but I still nodded.

He led me back down to the furniture store and toward the only man I'd seen in this country who was bigger than me.

"This is friend," the old man said.

"Hi," I said, with a smile.

"Buy something. Now." The big guy said.

I stayed away from the furniture because, of course, and I made my way through the knick knacks and souvenirs. Almost everything was made of marble and looked like it would break in my suitcase. I found a small glass hookah with etched-in red camels that said "Tunisia" on it and picked that one. It cost the last of the money in my wallet.

"That not enough," the big man said. "You buy more."

I froze. I didn't have any more money but didn't want to make the Big Man angry. I opened my wallet to show him that it was empty. He whistled and a young boy, maybe twelve years old, pops up out of nowhere. The two speak in Arabic to each other and then the boy nodded, grabbed my hand, and once again, I was off running down the dark twisted streets of the Tunis medina. I didn't even try to catch of sense of where I was going, but somehow it felt like we were going deeper into and away from the bustling busy parts of the market. My heartbeat started to pick up its pace, but I was already well past the point of no return. Sure, I could break from the grip of this 12-year-old boy, but where would I go? I wasn't just on the other side of the world, I was on the other side of town from my hotel, in a labyrinth medina, and inside it somewhere far from any other tourist. I hadn't seen another tourist since the mosque. And the only people who could possibly show me how to get back to the mosque were this boy, the old man, and the fat, unfriendly Big Man.

The boy and I stopped a tiny ATM in a cubby hole in a dark alley. I took a deep breath and prayed the ATM would recognize my US bank account. In between struggling to navigate a French language ATM transaction, I thought to check my phone to see if I had enough service to call my bank in case it declined, but I had no bars. And as the ATM spit out dinars, I questioned why I would call my bank instead of literally anyone I knew back at the conference. But even if I had bars, what would I say? "I'm lost in the Tunis medina. No, I can't tell you where I am. Somewhere dark, without people?"

The boy raced me back to the furniture store and by then the Big Man had decided what I would buy. Two marble mosaic discs, one a picture of an olive tree, the other a fish. I didn't know it at the time, but these marble mosaic discs are quite common in Tunisia. But different cities have different designs. Palm trees, camels, etc. The olive tree and the fish are like ancient brand logos for Tunis.

After they wrapped and bagged my hookah and mosaics, everything was done. The Big Man shook my hand and smiled for the first time, and then we were all just awkwardly standing there. I could have left, but with no idea where I was, there was little chance I'd find my way out. The old man who brought me was talking in Arabic to one of the employees when I tapped his shoulder, gave him three dinar, and said, "Take me mosque?" He nodded and we were off again, running through darkened narrow streets.

When we get back to the mosque and the plaza, the old man brewed me tea with jasmine, for free, apparently.

"You come back Tunisia, yes?" He asked.

And like with so many other local Tunisians I would meet throughout that week, who opened their homes to me, who struggled through their broken English and my non-existent French or Arabic, who smiled while placing their arm alongside mine, to show me we had the same skin tone and were therefore family, like all these people, the old man couldn't just say good-bye, they all had to ask.

"You come back Tunisia, yes?"

And I said, to all of them, "Yes. I'll come back."

THE DAY HIKERS

LISA MONTAGNE

W hen she opened the door, the Englishman was dressed in a blue, button-down Oxford shirt neatly tucked into khaki shorts. The side utility pockets were empty except for a bulgy wallet. He had a red bandanna around his neck, and he wore Birkenstock sandals with athletic socks that ended mid-calf. All that was missing was a utility belt and one of those safari hard hats with mosquito netting. Maybe a butterfly net. They were in the suburbs of Los Angeles, not in the Saharan desert. And, how far he thought he could hike in Birkenstocks, she did not know.

The Englishman was fair with blue eyes and thick, dark hair that lay across his head in attractive disarray. His hands relaxed in his front pockets, and he rocked back on his heels. Just shy of a stand-in for Mr. Darcy, he was closer to a chubbier, young Hugh Grant. She half expected him to greet her with a hearty "Cheerio," but he just said "Hi," chasing it with a substantial smile, bearing his large, white teeth at her.

They met through mutual friends and been on a few dates. When she asked him to go on a hike with her, he said, "Sure."

"Yay! It's one of my very favorite things!" she exclaimed, stopping herself from clapping, afraid to show too much enthusiasm. She settled for being pleased that he took an interest in one of her passions.

On their previous dates, he had been dressed in a soft, black t-shirt, snugly fitting jeans, and polished leather loafers or button-down shirt and nicely tailored slacks. He seemed perfectly normal, handsome even. But now he was on her doorstep looking like one of those Disneyland Jungle Cruise guides. *But who am I to judge?* she thought, smiling a little to herself. *He is good looking enough to get away with it.*

As a teenager, she had been a long-distance runner, but in college her running habit turned into frequent hikes in the county, state, and national parks around Southern California. They met at her apartment so she could drive them to one of the trailheads. He was new to the area, a recent transplant from London.

She had on navy-blue running sweats with her alma mater, UCLA, in lettering down the sides, a tank top, a thin blue hoodie, and sturdy sneakers. Her small backpack contained a bottle of water, a pair of binoculars, her wallet, and a cherry Chapstick. Her long, brown hair was pulled back into a practical ponytail. She was not tall, and her body was athletic rather than slender.

For their hike, she planned a route through a small ravine and up a range of hills between Malibu and the Valley. The map showed them arriving at the top of a high hill after an hour of walking from the trailhead. At the summit, they would have a first-class view of the Pacific Ocean. *But no.* He had also studied a map and wanted to go inland in the opposite direction to a different trailhead in the Angeles National Forest out towards Lancaster/Palmdale.

"We'll be able to see so much more of the surrounding

topography from there," he said. In his accent. *More than the Pacific Ocean,* she thought. *Huh.* He tossed the word "topography" off as lightly as foam on a cappuccino. She narrowed her eyes at him for a few seconds.

Damn it. Why does he have to be so cute, she thought. She took a breath. Gesticulating like a caffeinated Italian, she attempted to make her case.

"Well, let's see," she began. "Your route will take at least an hour to reach by freeway. Then we will have to drive at least another hour, if not more, into the park. Part of it will be over paved roads, but part of it won't be, and the hike will take us into territory where there is a chance for brush fires at this time of year, and where there are coyotes, cougars, wild boars, and possibly even bears."

"Bears? Really? Surely not," he said in mock horror.

She rolled her eyes inwardly. She wasn't even crazy about the idea of encountering a pissed off deer or even a mildly vexed squirrel. A skunk would definitely not be good. And, at the location he chose, there would be no view of the ocean. They wouldn't even have a view of the city—just some foothills, a dry bit of dessert, and a horizon as flat as a prizefighter's nose. That trail wasn't for day hikers like them. She hadn't even packed snacks.

She finished her speech weakly with: "I really don't recommend it." She was used to people not taking her word for it, so she let it go.

What she wanted was to go on a pleasant, romantic walk in the hills with a beautiful view as the reward at the end of it. She imagined that they would kiss on the hilltop, while the ocean waves winked back at them in complicity. He would hold her tight, stroke her cheeks and hair. She would feel safe and relaxed pressed against his belly. Then, they'd hit a quiet, cool bar by the beach for a drink. That was her idea of a date.

Besides, she was hoping to get lucky with this guy before sunset.

But, since she had met the Englishman, he always knew the better route, the better restaurant, the better book. And, so far, she always let him think he was right. She wanted the Englishman to like her—it was simple as that. When she spoke her mind in the past, the consequences were not good. People melted down like wax figures, faded like ghosts in the social mist, or worse, spoke back. In college, one guy told her she was not dating material because she was too smart, too capable, too much.

"You intimidate me," that guy had said, "I'd never date you."

Locked in perpetual conflict with her father, her mother wanted a better life for her daughter. So, her mother emphasized that a woman's instincts, opinions, and talents were nothing compared with "getting along" and "finding a way to please." So, when politely offered logic or witticisms failed, she rolled over like a beta dog. She made on-the-spot decisions to appease the person in front of her, everyone from her father to grocery store clerks. Conflict cost too much. Now, there was the Englishman standing in her living room.

"Come on," he said, pointing at the map. "We just pop right over this way. Look here. We won't even be that far from the blasted Hollywood sign."

She sighed to herself. He was quite wrong, of course. They would not be able to see the Hollywood sign from there. She had experienced this with English tourists before. The scale of maps in California simply did not equate with the scale of England. "Popping down the road" in England was literally a few miles over well-used paved roads with a pub every fifty feet; in California, it could mean many hours of back-breaking driving for hundreds of miles over empty terrain without seeing so much as a dried-up billboard sign, especially in the mountains. Or, without careful planning, a "quick drive" could mean hours stuck in traffic. One did not "pop" anywhere in California. But those tourists never listened. One incident ended with baby puke in her lap.

"Come on, it's more of a challenge," he said, cheerily. "An adventure!"

"Okay," she said, rolling over like a beta dog she was. *Keep it together,* she thought. *Remember, you want the Englishman to like you. You want to be dating material.*

"That's my girl!" Again, he laid on a big grin that made his dimples crinkle. He gave her a quick peck on the cheek and swept past her out the door.

She steered the car east instead of west. Overhead, there was a clear sky and a slight breeze. It was 70 degrees Fahrenheit at 11 am. It couldn't be a more perfect day for a hike by the ocean. She shook her head slightly in regret, but she headed towards the trailhead he chose.

"We should turn here," he said, after they had been driving for over two hours. She was right. That's where the dirt road started.

"I'm not sure that my car will do well on that road," she remarked, unsure if they should continue. She had an ancient four-door sedan made for wide Southern California freeways, unsuitable for off-roading.

"It's just a little bit down this way," he said, pointing ahead.

"Okay, but there's no reason that we can't just walk from here," she suggested.

"There are no trees to shade the car here. Let's drive in further," he urged her. He seemed to be having fun, still clearly uninterested in her ideas on the matter.

She eased the sedan onto the dirt road. It was slow going at

5 miles an hour. They bucked along as she avoided potholes and large rocks. They could have walked faster.

"Let's just get out here," she said. "This is a pretty spot."

"Yes, maybe," he replied. "But if we don't go to the actual trailhead, we may miss the path to that ripping view." He was now looking at a paper map, a guide to the park he'd printed out, because there was no cell reception there.

Yes, a "ripping" view of "topography," she thought. *Come on, keep your opinions to yourself. You can do it.*

At the trailhead, the marker read 2,000 feet above sea level. According to the sedan, it was 91 degrees Fahrenheit. She had already drained her water bottle, and she wasn't even out of the car yet. One pickup truck was parked nearby, but otherwise the park was deserted. Not many people came out hiking in the big parks at that time of year in 90-degree weather. They were all at the beach.

"Ah, isn't this lovely?" he declared, a little forced, breathing in the warm, dry air. He screwed an incongruous baseball cap down tight on his head. His thick hair stuck out at random angles from underneath.

"Oh, yes," she lied. "Quite lovely." She was still smarting from missing a generous view of the ocean and enjoying cool, fresh air.

She surveyed the area. It was late September, and so the ground was dry and cracked, and the grass was as brown as moth's wings. There had been no rain for at least five months. Their feet kicked up dust as they walked toward the start of the path, which was marked with football-size stones.

About 100 yards up the trail, she could see that the Manzanita bushes, coyote brush, and cactus plants gave way to stands of trees. The trees were mostly scrubby, low pines, and large oaks the color of mud. Even though the oak trees grunted out green leaves for only a few months in the winter, she felt a deep affinity with them. As a child, she climbed these types of oaks in Ventura County. Nestled in their loving arms, she read books and daydreamed about tree fairies. Sometimes, she felt like an oak tree herself—stoic and wide in spirit, passing along her share of water to the greedy evergreens, surviving on the hope that next year might bring one more inch of rain.

Their destination was at the top of the mountain range spreading out in front of them. It was true; from the top, they would be able to see for hundreds of miles around, but it would take another hour or more to get up there. And, then it would take an hour or more to get back. Even though the sun would not set until after 6 PM, it would be almost dark by the time they got back to the car. The early fall days were shortening. They had run out of water. No sunscreen. No cell phone reception. Basically, no provisions. Stats said that over 2,000 people get lost every year in the U.S. wilderness. She trusted herself well enough, but she knew the Englishman did not know what he was in for despite her warnings. Maybe he would get tired. Surely, he couldn't last long in those sandals. Hopefully, he'd want to turn back before the coyotes wanted a snack.

There was a sharp incline where the trailhead began. She loved hiking, after all, so she eased up on the grip of her grudge.

"Let's race!" she said, taking off up the hill, outpacing him easily.

Puffing to catch his breath, he landed at the top of the hill twenty paces behind her, his socks now brownish red from trail dirt. His tidy English façade was fraying as droplets of sweat appeared from under his hat. Still, he seemed undaunted. She dared not ask how the Birkenstocks were holding up.

They stood side by side and looked down.

"Now, this *is* quite nice," he said.

At their feet was a small but classic meadow. Oaks, pines,

and fir trees surrounded it. The wildflowers from the previous spring were long gone. There was mostly thistle weed and dry grass, but it was "quite nice" just the same.

Maybe Snow White and her gang will show up next, she thought. *At least Snow White can control wild animals by singing at them.* She didn't think singing at coyotes or bears would be much of a deterrent, but, at this point, buoyed by the beautiful meadow, she was determined to carry on up the trail if the Englishman was.

As they headed down a slight dip in the path that led across the meadow, she said, "Come on, old man, get a move on." She patted him playfully and took him by the arm. She was finally starting to have a nice time.

"I say!" he exclaimed abruptly. "What is *that?*" He stopped short and pointed ahead about 50 yards. There was a shining band in the dirt across the trail. The sun sparkled off its surface like a mirage, but it was not a stream or even a puddle.

"Let me see," she said, as she brushed him aside to have a look. "I can't quite tell." She squinted and walked a few paces closer, pulling out her binoculars. "Hmm..." She cocked her head quizzically to the side, as she put the lenses up to her face.

"Oh," she said flatly. "I believe that is a snake. A very big one. An odd time for it to be out and about. It's so hot."

A snake, she thought. *Here we go.* The wildlife was stirring much earlier in the hot day than she expected. Here was her excuse to head back to the car. *Maybe it isn't too late to have that drink*, she mused.

"A snake!?" he blurted in disbelief. "Are you sure?" he asked, like he knew better. The sweat droplets now formed small rivers down the sides of his face, and sweat stains sprang from various locales on his shirt.

"Just because there are no snakes in Ireland doesn't mean there aren't ones here," she smirked. He just scowled and snatched the binoculars, still around her neck, knocking her towards him.

"Oh! I say," he exclaimed as he clapped to the lenses to his face, the string stretched taut between them.

"Well, guess we have had our adventure," she said, taking back the binoculars. "You can tell all your friends in London that you saw a big snake. We can head back now." She turned back down the trail. But he caught her arm and pulled her to face him. He bent over her until they were nose to nose.

"But isn't it dangerous?" he asked, whispering, gripping her forearms.

"Umm, yes," she replied, pulling away. "That's why we should head back down."

"But it could chase after us. Shouldn't we alert a ranger or something?" he said, looking around vaguely and then returning his gaze to the shining band across the trail.

"Like who? Ranger Smith? Lurking in the trees at the exact time we need him? It doesn't work that way out here," she quipped, her patience flagging again. "I suppose you want Yogi and Boo Boo to bring us a pic-a-nic basket, too. Goodness knows I could use one about now. Preferably one with a Champagne split in it."

"What kind of snake do you suppose it is?" he wondered, talking over her. He continued to be transfixed by it, as if he was staring at a car wreck on the other side of the freeway.

"It could be a California glossy snake," she offered. "Or, as my Grandmother used to call them a garden snake, but she misspoke. She meant 'garter' snake. Or, it could be a very fat rattlesnake, though I doubt it. I don't hear a rattle."

In high school, she'd done research on California's snakes because she went for long runs in the Conejo Valley hills. She had seen plenty of sidewinders charging slantways through the hills behind her childhood home. Whenever she heard a rattlesnake, she walked in the opposite direction. Because that's what people did.

"Well, then?" he asked.

"Well, what?"

"Have a look."

"What business is it of ours?" She stayed screwed to her spot on the trail, feeling less desperate for him to like her.

"I think we have a duty here," he said. She could see the gears working between his ears. "If we can save other hikers, we should. I mean, it might attack someone who walks right up on it, like we almost did."

"Save them from what? *ALL* the snakes?" she asked, hands on hips. She watched as he took slow, deliberate steps towards the snake in his Birkenstocks.

She followed him, annoyed. She peered at the snake through the binocular lenses again. She stopped short, "Golly, it IS a big one," she added. Intrigued, she walked a bit closer despite her misgivings. "I don't think I've ever seen such a long, fat one before, except in the zoo. It's kind of huge."

All the time they were looking at it, the snake just lay in the middle of the path. In fact, it was so still, it might already be dead. Or maybe it was just sunbathing. *Regardless,* she thought, *I'm sure it'd rather be left in peace.*

"Huh, if it's alive," she speculated, still considering the beast through the lenses, "it must have just eaten something. A big something, which made it sleepy. Sometimes, if they are frightened, they freeze up. They also have poor eyesight. Or maybe it's already dying..."she trailed off. "Oh, no. Not dead," she said, backing up. As if on cue, the snake had slithered a few inches, but went still again. She continued looking through the binocular lenses, mulling over the state of the sluggish snake. *What could possibly be wrong with it?*

The Englishman marched a few paces past her.

"Where are you going?" she asked.

"To kill it," he replied, keeping his eyes on the snake.

"Kill it?"

"With these." He held some large rocks in each of his hands. "I'm going to throw these stones at it. What if somebody else comes along and gets attacked? There could be children, or anyone. I think we have a duty here."

"Uhhh...." She was wavering. That snake was hardly hurting anyone. But what if the Englishman *was* right? Maybe they should "do their duty." The snake might be mostly dead, anyway. Maybe they would be putting it out of its misery. His intention hung in the air, and still she hesitated. *Remember, you want him to like you,* she reminded herself. She could also hear her mother saying, "Always listen to those older and wiser." *Was the Englishman wiser because he was older? Because he was someone other than herself?*

Finally, she realized his proposal was absurd. There were probably hundreds—even thousands—of snakes in that forest. Would they kill them all? A bullet of frustration shot up from her heart through her left temple. But like the snake, she was frozen in that spot by indecision.

Before she could stop him, he had already thrown the first stone at the snake from about twenty feet away. He crouched, ready to run. The first one missed. But the snake didn't seem to care there was an Englishman throwing stones at it. It was completely still.

"Keep back!" he ordered, holding out his arms as if to bar the way, playing the part that matched his outfit. He was a man on safari protecting tourists from a surprise attack.

The second stone hit its mark. Blood burbled up through the slick, shiny band of the snake's brownish-gray skin, forming a rivulet into the dirt. She couldn't understand why the snake didn't simply slither into the underbrush. He threw a third stone, which also hit its mark. The snake was bleeding from two spots now.

Move, damn you! What is the matter? This man is attacking you, she thought wildly. Was it weighed down by a meal? Afraid? Why didn't it run? Maybe it was simply confused. Like her. Maybe she wasn't a wise, unselfish oak after all; maybe she was just a half-dead (or perhaps just-sunbathing) snake minding its own business, vulnerable to attack by a know-it-all Englishman.

"It's not reacting," she observed in a low voice. "It's just lying there bleeding." The Englishman was not listening. She could have said that she was on fire, but he would not have heard her.

"Perhaps more stones," he said, gathering them with determined gestures like a long-armed crane over a building site.

"*More* stones?" she said, but still, he didn't hear her.

Blood was now gushing from the snake in several spots, seeping into the dirt. A wave of sadness surged inside her chest, collected, and rolled over her in a wave, like when she heard children crying in a grocery store, or when her parents bickered behind closed doors. Now, she truly regretted being there, blaming herself for letting it happen.

She wished the Englishman would just vanish. Her mind hurried through an imagined sequence of events, like a scene rushing at her out of a 3D movie screen: In a fierce movement, the snake lifted its head like a dignified python rising out of a snake charmer's basket. It focused a knowing gaze on the Englishman, hissing, ready to strike forward. But instead of charging forward, the snake called up a dozen stones of its own. They floated in the air like a crown around the snake's head. The stones hovered, and then, with a flick of its head, the snake ordered the stones to fly. Like a swarm of disturbed bees, the stones hurtled through the air at the Englishman, overwhelming him in a buzzing, dark cloud that ate him up. In her mind, she vanquished him. She meant, it—*the snake*—had vanquished him. Poof. Just like that, the Englishman was simply gone.

As this fantastical scenario struck her, the seconds ticked off—one, two, three, four...

But the Englishman was not gone. He was there, in reality, still chucking stones at the bleeding snake. No amount of wishing him away was going to get rid of him. She would have to do that for herself. *Sorry, Mother, I'm still single,* she would have to say on their next call.

Snapping back into the moment, she said, "No."

"What?" said the Englishman distractedly, as he focused on throwing another stone with increasing force. Another wound opened on the back of the snake.

"No!" she repeated. "Leave it. Just leave it." *That poor creature. What was this crazy guy doing?*

"But that bugger could cause somebody harm," the Englishman protested.

"Cause harm? It's just lying there. You can do what you want," she announced, "but I'm leaving right now with or without you." She turned her back on him. Five or six long beats passed as he stood perfectly still, his gaze still fixed on the snake, which remained unmoving on the trail.

"Okay," he finally said. "Okay. We should go. What a shame, though."

"A shame? Did you say a shame?" she said, whirling back around.

"Yes?" he replied unsurely. "I...I meant it was shame we didn't get to see the view at the top," he continued, pointing up the mountain..."the snake being in the way and all."

"In the way? You think *it* was in *our* way?"

"I mean, if we were sure it was dead, we could have kept going to the top. For the view."

She wanted to say that it was he who should be ashamed. She wanted to say that he was acting crazy. She wanted to say that he didn't know everything. She wanted to say that he should have listened to her and gone to the beach. She wanted to say that she was smart, that she knew things, a lot of things. She wanted to say that she was kind and good. That she was dating material, wife material. Worthy of being heard. Worthy of love. That he would be lucky to have her. *But nobody ever listens to be,* she sobbed to herself. *I'm too young, I'm too much, I'm not dating material...Damn it.*

Her cheeks burned because she could not say words like that out loud to him or to anyone. They stuck in her throat like sand filling a bucket. She could imagine elaborate scenes for disappearing a person. She could offer logic and information, wrapping her opinions in witty remarks so they landed easily. But her mother's refrain "Get along. Be pleasant. Don't make trouble" rang in her head on a playback loop.

She took one more look back at the poor creature bleeding into the dust.

"I'm so sorry," she whispered. Then she stalked away, the Englishman following her, still insisting it was a shame that they didn't make it to the top of the trail. During the two-hour ride back to L.A., the Englishman prattled on about various points of the "topography," but she was mostly silent. She may or may not have responded with one-word replies.

To block out the Englishman and her mother's voice echoing in her head while she drove, she got lost in these words of Henry David Thoreau that she remembered from *Walden*:

They were pleasant spring days, in which the winter of man's discontent was thawing as well as the earth, and the life that had lain torpid began to stretch itself...I saw a striped snake run into the water, and he lay at the bottom, apparently without inconvenience; perhaps because he had not fairly come out of the torpid state. It appeared to me that for a like reason men remain in their present low and primitive condition; but if they should feel the influence of the spring of spring arousing them, they would of necessity rise to a higher and more ethereal life.

She was determined from that day forward to rise to a higher and more ethereal life. If nobody ever joined here there, she no longer cared.

When they arrived back at her apartment, they sat in her car in the dark. She made no move to get out and neither did he. He turned to her with expectation.

All that she could manage was, "You know, you were going to get lucky tonight."

He raised his eyebrows at this.

"What do you mean *were* going to get lucky?" he asked, as if there was still a chance.

"I'm tired," she replied.

"Well, then, I'll call you," he concluded.

"Don't bother," she said, getting out of the car and heading towards her door. He stood on the sidewalk, watching her walk away, looking wounded, like he'd left the snake.

A few months later, she heard from mutual friends that the Englishman had proposed to a girl even younger than her. He would get his green card and be able to stay in the country. They married, bought a house in L.A. and had a baby. A few years later, rumors floated back to her that they got divorced. He had snapped, they said. He had beaten her up and threw her clothes out the back door, they said. He'd cheated on her, they said. She believed every word. She had narrowly escaped the fate of the snake, while this other girl clearly had not.

ONE SOLDIER TOO LATE

BENJAMIN WHITE

In the early 1980s before the Berlin Wall came down and the Iron Curtain fell, I was exiled by economics. When the government's trickle-down fiscal policies failed to financially irrigate the fields of South-Central Kentucky, a lot of farms were being auctioned off, my school money had run out, Main Street had been boarded up, and the banks were lending at 15% interest. No one could afford to leave the house.

In global politics, President Reagan was on a mission to outspend the Soviets, and the best offer anywhere was to accept the Veterans' Education Assistance Program and join the Army. Ronnie would have given me an $8,000 bonus if I had signed up for the infantry for four years. But I only wanted to serve two years, then get out, and go back to school.

Honestly, I wasn't really sold on the two years, but I went through the testing, passed the physical examination, and spoke with a career counselor. She tried her best to get me in for more than two years, saying I qualified for all the occupational specialties the Army offered, but on a two-year enlistment, she could only give me the infantry. I stood up with my no-thank-you face, but she reeled me back in with the lure of West Germany.

I was poor, not stupid, so I sat back down.

I made it to the 1st and 51st Infantry Battalion in Crailsheim, West Germany, a couple of days before my 22nd birthday. I was newly qualified as an 11-Charlie, Indirect Fire Infantryman and couldn't care less about operating the weapon of my specialty – a mortar. It was an obsolete weapon, and as soon as you popped off one round, the improved technology of the day could reverse-track the trajectory, pop off a much-more-advanced weapon, and wipe the mortar crew off the face of the Veterans' Education Assistance Program. That would have blown the deal.

But I was smart enough to know that my experience in West Germany was a gift from the United States, and given the economic problems being harvested in southern Kentucky, I deserved a gift. So, I played soldier during the hours I was required to play soldier, knowing that I was simply a tourist camouflaged as a warrior.

Ronnie's interest rates made the dollar a strong commodity, so exchanging them for Deutsche Marks was a financially great decision. I couldn't afford not to get out of the barracks and away from the base at Crailsheim where the local people had put up with soldiers for 40+ years and weren't as open to me as I was to receiving local hospitality. On weekends, I took the train to a small town called Gaildorf. As far as a typical tourist hotspot, it had extraordinarily little to offer. But as a gateway into German culture, it had everything I needed.

I was first taken to Gaildorf by another soldier, Blaine, who was also basically on a European vacation. He introduced me to that small town, and then he introduced me to Beatrix, a girl originally from East Germany. He called her Trixie. He was not really fixing me up with a German girl, and he had no romantic intentions for us. He was just politely helping me get more immersed in the local community.

Although my Vietnam veteran brother had given me strict instructions not to marry a *fraulein*, I was very much interested in local romance. I didn't deserve it, of course. Before joining the Army, I had broken up with my last girlfriend...in a letter... on her birthday. Not my finest hour. Nevertheless, I was ready to start over on another continent. So, what I actually deserved, and what I received, was Trixie.

My heart was open – young and open. I wasn't necessarily homesick; I was adjusting to Army life. While on-duty, I was meeting all the infantry requirements and found enough self-discipline to do what I was told. While off-duty, I used the time alone to reflect and find myself. So when I met Trixie, I was eager to bill myself as a rehabilitated romantic. But Trixie wasn't romantic.

Trixie was pregnant.

At first, I didn't know. How would I know? Why should I know? We were introduced under common social circum-stances: boy, this is girl; girl, this is boy. We met in the Number One Club in Gaildorf. I was alone because that is the common state of being an exile. At the time, I didn't know why she was also alone, but I accepted her apparent availability as a sign that time and distance had forgiven me for my past sins.

She seemed to be at the club out of habit more than anything else, experiencing the German nightlife. I loved the Number One Club for the same reasons she did, but now I had another reason to love the club. I went to see her.

Blaine saw right away what was happening to me. He saw me falling for her and felt obligated to let me know what he knew.

Trixie was pregnant.

I am sure he was telling me out of a sense of loyalty.

However, I am not sure if it was loyalty to me or loyalty to the father of the baby. The father was another American soldier who was waiting – anxiously – for the day he would leave Germany. He was within two weeks of transferring and would not budge from the barracks. Mother Army was protecting him, and his own band of brothers were not going to deny him his escape. They told Trixie he had already left the country. Blaine told me not to tell her anything different. I didn't have to; she never asked.

Trixie wasn't romantic...or idealistic.

I still don't know if it was chivalry, romance, stupidity, or just plain youthful ignorance – if not arrogance – but I didn't let Trixie know that I knew. I was still falling for her, enjoying every minute we spent together at the club.

Then on Labor Day 1983, Trixie and I met in passing on the street and spent the afternoon together in Gaildorf. It wasn't the last time I saw her, but it was the last time I was really with her.

And I needed her. She spoke English, probably better than I did, but she refused to rely on her second language to communicate with me. She exclusively spoke German to me, and I had to fill in the blanks between the few words I knew and the whole vocabulary I didn't. I admired her for kicking my language skills out of their comfort zone. That was, after all, part of my reason for taking the Army up on the opportunity to get out of Kentucky.

She smiled at my linguistic bungling, and I loved to see her smile.

On that Monday, as we walked around Gaildorf, I wanted to be nowhere else in the world. It wasn't about romance or sex or even trying to build any foundation for the future. It was a right-here, right-now situation, and I cherished those moments.

It was a chance for us to be away from our circle of friends and grow our own friendship.

Despite what I knew about her, or maybe *because* of what I knew about her, I was forced to measure my feelings. But she was beautiful, young, energetic, so she had my attention and my heart.

We walked by a storefront – it must have been a drug store – and in the window was a picture of a fully-developed fetus in a womb. She stopped and looked at the picture. In one of the few times she spoke English, she told me she wished she could go back to East Germany. She may have been talking out loud to herself, but it was in English, so I took it to be for my benefit. She gave no reason for her desire, so I jumped to conclusions about why anyone would want to go back to a communist country. As a matter of having taken an oath, I was an American soldier defending the west against Soviet invasion, so I was expected to hold my loyalties on the right side of the campaign. The communists, I reasoned, would not have thought twice about ending the pregnancy. We walked on without any more discussion about what she had said, or what I had silently projected as my understanding.

Then, we came up behind a woman pushing a baby carriage. Trixie picked up her pace, and I stayed with her, so we could pass the woman. Trixie seemed extremely interested in seeing the baby, but as we walked by, and looked into the carriage, there was no baby. The woman was just pushing an empty buggy. She may have been going to pick up her baby, taking the new carriage home, or had just purchased the carriage as a gift. We didn't know. There was just no baby.

"*Kein Baby,*" Trixie smiled.

"Where's the baby?" I asked her.

She shrugged. I shrugged back. She smiled. I smiled back.

And beyond those nonverbal exchanges, I didn't think about it too deeply.

"*Und jetzt?*" She asked after we had passed the last shop on the street.

"And now?" I tried to impress her by knowing a simple phrase.

She smiled, and I led her across the street to continue our conversation. The September sun was sinking faster than I wanted it to. I knew she would be going home soon, and I would have to head back to Crailsheim.

One afternoon walking through a small German town gave me no reason to claim a deepened relationship with Trixie, so my feelings were just pesky romantic notions needling me. Still, I did not want to go up the hill to the train station without her. Being alone I could take. I deserved being alone. But loneliness was different. It came with a sense of loss.

In what I would later speculate was a ploy to find a father (and a benefactor) for her child, she asked me a question. I pieced together the words I knew.

"*Gasthaus...Crailsheim...Donnerstag?*"

I wasn't quick enough to translate the question about meeting her at a guest house in Crailsheim, and she took my hesitation as a linguistic issue. She forcefully went through the days of the week until I understood Thursday. Although I was going to say yes, I didn't say it quickly enough, so she changed the subject (if not her mind), and we kept walking.

We stopped on the sidewalk where the shops ended. Trying to come up with a way to get back to the invitation, I was clowning around singing and dancing like Joe Cocker. She smiled and reached up to touch the back of my head, when the cuff of her jacket poked me in the eye making my contact lens pop out. Then, I was contorting my face like Joe Cocker hoping my contact was still in my eye. It wasn't there. It had fallen out.

It was getting dark, but she had a disposable lighter, so she lit it and held it while I hopelessly searched the sidewalk. I shrugged it off as just another lost contact, but noticed she was concerned. With sincerity, I told her not to worry about it.

Then, in a pure display of bad timing, I leaned in to kiss her, and she pulled away. I nodded and looked into her eyes with a cross between understanding, hurt, and absolute longing. We continued our walk around the block.

Our day ended shortly after that. We said goodbye, and I went back up the hill to the *bahnhof,* catching the last train to Crailsheim.

The next time I saw her, I was wearing United States Army-issued Birth Control Glasses (BCGs) because my replacement contacts had not yet arrived from the states. She smiled when she saw me, the glasses validating that I had actually lost a contact. She may have thought it had been a ploy to get her close enough to kiss. I don't know. I was coming out of the Number One Club, and she was going in. She was with a boy – a German boy. I always took that to mean she had had enough of Americans in general, and of American soldiers, specifically.

Fate and the future have a secret relationship that we struggle to understand throughout our lives. Her mature fate had nothing to do with my immature future, and her intuitive future had nothing to do with the uncertainty of my fate. But memory holds it all together in terms of "what if." I never saw her again, but I have often wondered what would have happened if I hadn't been an exile who also turned out to be one soldier too late.

WHEN I DREAM I DIE

MARGO MCCALL

Greta didn't usually go out with clients—in fact, she never had—but when she encountered Howard in the elevator, she decided to make an exception. And now, driving to Manhattan Beach to meet him for dinner, she couldn't stop thinking about how he'd somehow known about that secret spot on her neck where the nerve endings were close to her skin.

She didn't trust chemistry because it usually meant there was some kind of childhood projection at work, or at least that's what her self-help books advised. But she did believe in synchronicity. The books said it was okay to believe in that.

If she hadn't left her cell phone in her car, she wouldn't have followed him into the elevator after his meeting with her boss, Sally. If she hadn't dropped her car keys, he wouldn't have bent down to retrieve them. If she hadn't gotten that crescent moon tattoo on her calf, he wouldn't have asked if she had others. And if she hadn't showed him the tiny star below her ear, he wouldn't have gone for her neck like it was home.

Something had happened while descending five floors of a nondescript office building in Santa Monica. When the doors opened and they walked in, they were strangers. And when the doors opened and they walked out, they were something else. Lightning-fast connections like that were rare.

Greta arrived at the beachside restaurant where they agreed to meet just as Howard was slipping his keys to the valet. More synchronicity, she told herself. But when he moved in for a hug, his phone chirped before their bodies touched.

"Excuse me," he mouthed. "Important call."

In a burst of multi-tasking, Howard gestured for her to enter the restaurant, announced their arrival to the hostess, and wrapped up the call just as they were being seated.

He flashed her a smile. She wondered if he was trying to impress her by how wide his mouth could stretch. Or maybe he was just demonstrating he had a good dentist.

"Sorry about that—flying to Boston in the morning." He reached for her hands and squeezed them. "Long time no see."

"Yes," Greta said. "Almost an hour."

She'd had a general impression of him from the elevator—a handsome, broad-shouldered man in an expensive suit—but she already knew secrets, like how he smelled beneath the cologne. Now, in the watery pink of sunset, she was getting a deeper look: boyish eyes, ruddy skin, trimmed eyebrows, manicured nails.

"I could use a drink after that hellish traffic," he said. "How about you?"

"Yes, definitely cocktail hour. Or should we have wine?"

"Impressive wine list," he said, perusing the menu. "Do you like red? White?"

"Definitely red. And you?"

"Definitely red," he said. "They've got a Williamette Pinot or a Paso Robles Grenache. Let's ask the server which they recommend."

"Excellent idea."

It felt like a first date. Without the usual tension, thanks to their elevator ride. But they were going through first-date rituals. Establishing common ground. Finding out what the other person liked. The wines he suggested were a hundred dollars a bottle, demonstrating that he was generous and financially secure. And by agreeing with his suggestion, she was conveying her pleasant nature and supportiveness.

The server recommended the Pinot and took their dinner orders—skirt steak for him, vegetable risotto for her, half-dozen oysters for them.

Greta suddenly worried she could get fired for going out with a client.

"So, what do you do with the agency?" she asked.

"I consult on Sally's biotech companies. Navigating drug trials and approvals."

"Oh good, so you're not actually a client. You work for her, like me."

Under the table, his hand touched her leg. "Worried about crossing a line?" he asked, raising an eyebrow. "And what do you do for Sally?"

"Pitching, press releases."

"Do you have a degree in public relations?" he asked, initiating the degree-comparison portion of their date.

"I have a couple of degrees in psychology, and a certificate in marketing." She was keeping it purposefully vague, and though she didn't ask him about his degrees, he told her anyway.

"I went to Brown for my undergrad in biology, then got my MS and PhD from Columbia and my MBA from Pepperdine. I also did a postdoc at UC San Diego."

OK, so he was smart. An overachiever.

"Sure you've got enough degrees?" she asked.

The server brought their bottle of wine and a silver dish of oysters on ice—Glidden Points from Maine, Malpeques from Prince Edward Island, and James Rivers from Virginia. Howard picked up a Malpeque, and after anointing it with lemon and horseradish, slipped it between her lips. The horse-radish exploded in her sinuses and her mouth filled with the taste of ocean. She wasn't used to being fed.

The sun was slipping into the ocean by the time the server removed the dish laden with empty oyster shells, and the inter-rogation about past relationships commenced. Yes, she'd been married. Ten years, Greta told him, all of them happy until right at the end.

Howard had been divorced for five. "She had no marketable skills," he said of his ex-wife, with no trace of rancor. "But she was a good mother to my children."

"How did you manage all those years of study while raising kids?" Greta asked.

"Oh well, my wife used to work. And we lived cheap. When we were at Columbia, we lived in a very sketchy part of Harlem."

"I've lived in bad neighborhoods, too. Hollywood. Down-town L.A.," Greta said. "Pre-gentrification."

He reached across the table to refill her wine glass, then said, "One of our neighbors shot his wife at one place we lived."

Greta's eyes widened. "Oh my God."

"We heard what we thought were firecrackers. Then screaming."

"What did you do?"

"My wife hid in the closet with our baby while I called 911."

"Did you see the body?"

"I saw them wheel out the body bag. And I caught a glimpse of what was left of her head. Quite a spray pattern of brain matter and bone on the ceiling." He paused. "Anyway, we were happy to lose those neighbors. Their arguments kept waking the baby."

The server deposited their entrees, but Greta no longer felt like eating. The rest of their conversation was a blur. When the check came, he paid, and she thanked him.

"Want to go for a walk on the pier?" he asked.

She wasn't sure what she was feeling. It was always like this, her emotions out of reach until hours, sometimes days, later, when they popped up with strange intensity. She was more in touch with other people's feelings than her own.

"Sure," she said hesitantly. "But I don't want to keep you out late with your early-morning flight."

He wrapped an arm around her shoulder as they strolled into the shadowy twilight. "I'd much rather be with you than go to Boston.Plus, I hardly ever sleep."

"Do you still dream?" she asked.

By then, they were halfway down the pier, leaning on the railing, staring at the ghostly breakers churning toward shore.

"I dream that I'm dead," he said.

"What do you mean?"

"I leave my body."

"That doesn't mean that you're dead."

"What else could it mean?" he asked worriedly.

"It could mean your subconscious is trying to tell you something."

"What is it trying to tell me?"

"Oh, I don't know. That you're working too hard maybe. Or ignoring your needs."

"I am working too hard. Sometimes I just wish I could..." His voice trailed off.

He suddenly grabbed her hand and shoved it inside his mouth. This was what a vagina must feel like, she thought.

Warm and wet and slippery. It was weird having part of her body inside someone else's.

She'd been about to tell him about her own dreams, the night terrors that left her sweaty and afraid. Sometimes she was being chased down a dark street. Or driving off a cliff in her car. The worst ones were kissing someone and having them suddenly transform into a fanged monster who wanted to kill her.

It was something she'd have to reveal if she ever slept with anybody, so they'd be less alarmed when she woke up screaming. But in the year since her divorce, she hadn't slept with anyone. With the help of her counselor, she was trying to move on. And so, even though something seemed off about Howard, she forced herself to proceed. Maybe she was just projecting her uncertainty onto a perfectly decent man. She'd have to see what her feelings said when they announced themselves in her dreams.

The next evening, Howard called from Boston. She'd just washed her face and was lying on the bed reading Clarissa Pinkola Estes' *Women Who Run with the Wolves,* a book her counselor said could help her connect to her inner power.

"I can't stop thinking about you," he said.

"How was your day? Any meetings?"

"Yes, I had a very important meeting. But with you on my mind, it was hard to concentrate."

"Shouldn't you be asleep by now? It's nearly two in your time zone."

"I took 35 milligrams of Ambien. Just waiting for it to kick in."

"Well, sweet dreams," she said. She wanted to get back to her book.

"Give me something to dream about."

She considered how the surf had gleamed white in the

moonlight as they'd walked on the pier. "Dream of waves," she said and hung up.

That night she dreamt of someone pointing a gun at her head, and it was scary enough to wake her. During her married years, when she'd woken with her heart beating hard and a garbled cry coming from her lips, her husband had been there to hold her. But now she only had the dream-analysis process she'd learned at the C.G. Jung Institute workshop.

Turning on the light, she opened her journal, and wrote down the symbols that appeared, and her associations with them. The gun symbolized power, male energy, a phallus, death. The associations attached were terror and powerlessness. If dreams were messages from the soul, as Jung said, what was her soul trying to tell her? Was Howard dangerous? Or was her dream just a reaction to him pursuing her?

It was a busy week at work, and Greta found herself taking the stairs instead of the elevator. She hoped it would give her distance to make up her mind about this man she'd just met. It didn't help that he wouldn't quit texting her.

"I like you a lot," he texted before his return flight. "Can hardly wait to see you."

"Have a good flight," she responded, not sure what else to say.

She didn't hear from him for almost a full day, then he texted her from Washington, D.C.: "Want to see you so bad. Have meeting Saturday, but are you free Saturday night?"

Greta took a while to answer, then nervously pecked out a reply: "K, will leave it open."

But after he hadn't called by Saturday afternoon, she went to a movie with her single friend, Nancy. When Greta first started dating, Nancy had given her advice. Always meet in a public place. Be careful about giving out personal information. Don't invite them to your place until you trust them. Nancy had listened patiently to Greta's reports on her first few bad dates since her divorce. The narcissist who wouldn't stop talking about himself. The grieving son who cried about his lost mother. The bitter man still blaming his parents for a bad childhood.

Now, Greta longed to ask her, "Has a guy ever put your hand in his mouth?" and "Is it a bad sign if a guy talks about a woman getting her head blown off?" But she was trying to figure things out on her own.

Howard texted her Sunday night: "Off to NY in the a.m. Thinking of you." Greta ignored him. She was reading *Bluebeard*. She was at the point where the wife disobeys her husband's orders and uses the forbidden key to open a locked room containing his previous wives' severed heads. Bluebeard was just about to cut off his current wife's head to punish her for her curiosity when Greta's phone rang. It was Howard.

"Why are you ignoring me?" he said in an agonized tone.

"What?" she asked, feeling annoyed. "We don't even know each other."

"You know I'm a good kisser, right?"

She thought about how he'd jammed her hand into the warm cave of his mouth. And more problematic, how he'd asked her to keep Saturday night open, then flaked without explanation.

"You won't hurt me, will you?" His voice had an Ambien slur.

"Sorry, I have to go," she said.

She returned to her book. Clarissa Pinkola Estes was explaining the moral of the Bluebeard story. A naïve young woman ignores her gut feeling and marries a serial killer, then she is saved from having her head cut off by her sisters. However, Greta didn't have any sisters. And now that her parents had retired to Arizona, not even any family nearby.

She hated how women were always being threatened, maimed, or killed in fairy tales. Like the Handless Maiden, whose father cut off her hands with an axe in a deal with the devil to become rich. But it wasn't just in fairy tales. Women were raped and killed on TV and in movies all the time. Not to mention in real life.

That night the tables were turned. At least in her dreams. She was the one doing the killing, strangling someone, possibly Howard, with her bare hands. When she woke up, her entire body was vibrating. And she recognized the feeling. Anger. She was making progress.

A couple of weekends later, Howard arrived at her door with two dozen roses. He thrust the cellophane-wrapped flowers toward her. "They're Rainforest-safe," he assured her. "I couldn't decide whether to get red or pink, so I got both."

The air between them prickled with energy. The minute he crossed the threshold he went right for the weak spot on her neck, but she pushed him away. She needed to put the roses in a vase of water. And there were dinner reservations at eight. She'd ignored a week's worth of texts and calls from him, hoping he'd go away. But he was relentless. Finally, she called him up and let him have it.

"I am so, so, very sorry," he'd said, sounding on the verge of tears. "I haven't slept more than a few hours a night in weeks, and I'm afraid it's made me a little crazy. Please let me make it up to you by taking you to dinner."

She'd let herself be persuaded, but as they drove to the restaurant, she wished she hadn't given in to his pressure. If the evening didn't go well, she could always Uber back to her place and not answer the door if he followed her there. She hated that part of dating—that part of being a woman. Always having to be aware of potential escape routes should things get dicey.

But so far, they were having fun. The restaurant was like

the inside of someone's home, the light soft and inviting, the smell of cooking coming from the kitchen. The hostess seated them at a corner table by the window and they ordered dirty martinis. Greta got the fried green tomatoes and Howard got the seafood gumbo. He offered her a taste of his gumbo, and she reciprocated by placing a slice of tomato on his side plate.

Howard said he'd gotten some sleep. Ten straight hours. And now felt more like himself. "Thank you for giving me another chance," he said more than once.

On the way back to her house, he kept touching her legs. She felt like she was in a porno movie. He seemed to be having trouble breathing, so she unhooked his fingers and placed his hand on his thigh. His slacks felt foreign and rough. They were probably expensive, some sort of silk wool blend. When they pulled up in front of her house, she said, "Thanks for the fun evening," and started getting out of the car to see how he would react.

"Just joking," she said after his eyes widened with disappointment. "I guess you can come in for a nightcap."

After the martinis, neither of them needed anything more to drink, so their nightcap was two glasses of water. She didn't feel drunk, but she must have been, because there were gaps of time. Like how did she get from offering him a glass of water to kissing him on the couch? And then they were lying on her bed with their clothes on. The walls shimmered with candlelight and Leonard Cohen's voice floated in from the living room.

"I adore you," he breathed. He repeated it like a mantra, whispering the words into her ear until it sounded like he was speaking a foreign language, "Iadoru...Iadoru."

Then he suddenly sat up and wanted to go home.

"Help me find my wallet," he said, staggering around, a befuddled mess.

"You OK to drive?" she asked. "Is everything all right? Why do you feel you have to go home?"

He murmured something incomprehensible, and after shoving his wallet in his back pocket, hurried toward the door.

"Let's go for a hike tomorrow," he said brightly. "I'll call you."

After he left, she sat outside on the back stairs and looked up at the sliver of moon. She felt like the hapless heroine of a romantic comedy. Inside, Leonard Cohen gave way to Moby. She turned off the music and went to bed. In the morning, Howard texted her while she was in the garden tending her tomatoes.

"I'll call you later," he said. When she called him back, he didn't answer, so she blocked him. That night, she dreamed she was dancing in a field of flowers, the sunshine warm on her back. She was alone and filled with contentment. There was no one trying to kill her. No darkness, only light. The warm, happy feeling stayed with her as she woke and began another day.

THE HEART SWINDLER

WENDY LANE

I n the middle of January, an officious envelope arrived in the mail with OPEN IMMEDIATELY on the front, like one of those sweep-stakes announcements. It was a summons for jury duty. *Bad timing*, I thought. A snowstorm was predicted that would plummet our Minnesota temperatures to sub-zero.

The Defendant

For many years, Li Mei Ziyang worked seven days a week, meeting potential clients from China who wanted to settle in Santa Clara, California. She was born in China, then moved to the United States. With a graduate degree in business economics, she was uniquely positioned to be a real estate agent for Chinese immigrants who, like her, sought prosperity. She named her business Laughing Waters, Inc., and it grew rapidly.

An attractive woman, with shoulder length, shiny black hair and a petite figure, her flawless skin belied her actual age.

She chose not to have children, instead building her business and giving back to her community. At 51, she aspired to find a partner to share the good life she created. A little fun, sex, adventure, romance, and, if she was lucky, even love. She started her search on a dating website.

Three years later, instead of gazing into the eyes of her beloved, she sat in a Minnesota courtroom facing a jury as the defendant in a criminal trial. She must have thought, *What happened to my dream of a better life? How is it I find myself here, under arrest, on trial as a criminal?*

Monday, January 28

The morning was brisk when I arrived at Ramsey County courthouse, an imposing twenty-story, limestone Art Deco skyscraper built during the Great Depression in downtown Saint Paul. Its historic grandeur impressed upon me that people's lives were at stake here. One level below the main floor, bronze elevator doors opened to the jury room. The large, rectangular space had capacity for 120, and it was full.

I was sixty-three-years old, white, lesbian, and married. I wondered how my identity or appearance would work for or against me in jury selection. The jury manager, a congenial, authoritative, tall, and slightly overweight black man, loudly announced:

"Bring your summons with you every day. Court starts at 9:30 each morning. If there are enough jurors for scheduled cases, those remaining are sent home on call. Your summons group number identifies you. Call the phone number on your summons any time after 5 p.m. A voicemail will state which group numbers must report the next morning. Call in daily."

He turned back to us and added sternly, "Do not leave this room unless you need to use the bathroom."

I thought, *This is a taste of how rigid jail must be.*

With logistics addressed, everyone looked bored or tired. I scanned the room and noticed my former hair stylist, Brandon. I sat down by him.

"Hi, Wendy."

We chatted in hushed voices, while others played games on their tablets or texted on cell phones. The overhead lights felt harsh. A few were slumped in chairs with eyes closed. We waited.

The jury manager dismissed us at 11 a.m. I grumbled about having to go out in the cold again, said goodbye to Brandon, and called my spouse Andrea to pick me up.

Tuesday, January 29

At 8:00 a.m. I dialed the jury duty number, and a woman answered, informing me, "We need jurors today, so you must come in." The weather channel announced twelve-below zero with a wind chill of thirty-eight below. Those temps cause frostbite on exposed skin in ten minutes. Andrea and I share a car, so she drove me to the courthouse. We piled on layers before leaving home.

Sitting next to Brandon again, I heard both of our names called for a trial. A total of twenty-two jurors split themselves between elevators and rode to the 13th floor. Outside the courtroom, the judge's assistant announced, "This is a criminal trial, so you must shut off your cell phones prior to entering."

He handed us each a lanyard labeled "Juror." He added, "Wear this everywhere in the courthouse to prevent people from talking to you about the case." I quickly sent Andrea a text to let her know I was going offline, then shut down my phone.

In the rear of the courtroom, we sat on parallel rows of carved, exotic-wood benches. The judge, a tall, distinguished black man with graying hair, stood behind an elevated podium at the front of the room. He introduced himself as presiding Judge Gene Matthewson.

Li Mei Ziyang sat at a table in front of the judge. Her head was down, and she sniffled, wiping tears from her eyes with a tissue. The judge introduced her as Ms. Ziyang, the defendant at the center of this trial.

A white man in his fifties with a muscular build in a fitted business suit sat next to Ms. Ziyang. The judge introduced him as Mr. Ken Vaurin, criminal defense attorney and Ms. Ziyang's lawyer. Another white man in a conservative gray suit was identified as Mr. William Fitch, Assistant Ramsey County Attorney for the state, criminal division. Mr. Fitch was older than Mr. Vaurin, had silver hair, a slender build, and wore glasses. Both attorneys eyed each juror closely as the judge spoke to us.

To the right of the table were the three-tiered rows of empty seats where twelve jurors and two alternates would sit. We were told to stand, raise our right hands, and accept the oath.

Judge Matthewson read Ms. Ziyang's criminal charge: "Swindle and theft of stolen property, then transferred and received as stolen property, valued at over $230,000. The case is the State of Minnesota vs. Li Mei Ziyang. There will be nine witnesses called."

As defined in Minnesota Statute section 609.52, subdivision 2(4), theft by swindle occurs when a person, "whether by artifice, trick, device, or any other means, obtains property or services from another person" under a false premise about the value or true nature of the goods. Theft by swindle is a felony offense.

The judge's assistant read aloud the names of potential jurors. I was called, Brandon was not. In a solemn tone, the judge said, "The burden of guilt is on the state to prove; the defendant is innocent until proven guilty."

My seat faced Ms. Ziyang directly. I was uncomfortable looking at her, so I focused on the judge or lawyers instead. I couldn't imagine what she must be feeling and didn't know what I was about to hear.

The judge informed us, "The lawyers have the opportunity to challenge jurors for dismissal. Don't take it personally if you are challenged and dismissed." Their questions included whether a member of our immediate families was involved in law enforcement, if we or family members had been arrested, tried for a crime, or participated in a trial previously.

Mr. Vaurin asked if any of us didn't want to be a juror. I wondered, *Does that matter?* An older woman seated to my right had a soft, slow way of speaking, drawing out her words and mumbling. The judge had asked her to repeat what she said because he couldn't hear or understand her. She raised her hand to report she had ADHD, and it was hard for her to focus.

Mr. Vaurin asked, "What happens when it is difficult for you? Is it hard to pay attention to details? Does your mind wander?"

She replied quietly, "Yes. I was homeless at one point and sitting still is difficult for me."

Immediately, both lawyers stood up to confer with the judge. After a couple of minutes, the judge turned to her and said, "You are dismissed from this case."

Before we left for the day, the judge glared at each potential juror and instructed, "You can't speak to anyone involved in the case. Not to each other, nor to anyone you know. And you can't search or post on the internet about the trial. You may only say you are prospective jurors. Do you agree to do this?" We did.

Wednesday, January 30

That morning the car radio announced the shutdown of schools, retail stores, medical clinics, and public transportation. Cancellations and flight delays were reported at the airport. There was a thin layer of ice, called black ice, that is difficult to see on the road, causing many accidents. But the trial carried on.

The day began with more questions from the defendant's lawyer. He was excruciatingly slow. Mr. Vaurin reminded me of professional athletes on TV who stumble through postgame interviews because they are uncomfortable with public speaking. He was unskilled in framing questions. Addressing the group, he asked, "Do you have any problem considering Ms. Ziyang innocent, regardless of whether she testifies or not?" His open-ended question created some confusion as to how we should respond. No-one said anything but many looked perplexed. After a moment he said, "Can you raise your hand if you think she is guilty if she declines to speak for herself?" Not a hand went up.

I looked at Ms. Ziyang's face and tried to guess what she must have been thinking. *Did she want to testify? Was she sad, angry, or worried?* Her face appeared serious but otherwise emotionally neutral. *Did she feel confident in Mr. Vaurin as her representative? Did she have a choice?* She scanned our faces carefully, too. *What impression did I give her?*

Mr. Vaurin reminded us, "Ms. Ziyang was crying yesterday when you entered the courtroom. Did you feel sorry for Ms. Ziyang or did anyone think Ms. Ziyang was faking her tears to gain your sympathy?" No-one said anything or raised a hand. I repeated the question to myself, *Was she faking?* I had not thought so before, but now Mr. Vaurin had planted the idea in my mind. I wasn't sure but didn't raise my hand to share this uncertainty. I considered all the times in my life when people have spoken for me, about me or over me. Rarely did they accurately represent or understand me. I would not have selected Mr. Vaurin as my lawyer.

Mr. Vaurin asked questions that revolved around cell phones, computers, email accounts, use of the internet, phishing scams, wire transfer of funds, electronic banking, and internet dating.

After lunch the lawyers decided who would serve on the jury. The judge's assistant called fourteen people, twelve jurors and two alternates. I was selected, and then my friend Brandon was added. He replaced the dismissed woman. The judge didn't tell us who would be alternates. Remaining potential jurors were dismissed. The jury was a mixture of races, genders, and ages. I felt honored and excited to be selected. I wanted to know more about Ms. Ziyang, the crime committed, and the trial process. I also dreaded the days ahead that would consist of sitting still, while being forced to listen carefully to endless waves of details.

The Fix

At last, Mr. Fitch, the prosecuting attorney, gave his opening statement and summarized a very sad story. Ms. Ziyang was a realtor in California, and the property market there was quite hot. She made a lot of money. Sadly, love was missing from her life, so she joined an online dating service and connected with a man named Morucci.

Morucci's profile included several pictures. His profile was projected on a screen for us to view. Ms. Ziyang didn't realize they were copies of celebrity photos stolen from the web. Mr.

Fitch informed us they were pictures of Andy Cohen, a famous radio and talk show host, writer, and producer. *How bold or stupid does someone have to be to use a recognizable person's photo?* One profile picture was a close-up, with a dog resting its head on his shoulder. The dog appeared devoted to his owner. Morucci looked to be an attractive and approachable middle-aged white man who liked dogs and was about the same age as Ms. Ziyang. Within weeks of connecting online with Morucci, she confessed love for him.

Morucci told her he was originally from Oregon, but currently on business in Dubai. He was quite well off financially and owned a gemstone business. His company ran into some trouble. He needed financial assistance, and requested she loan him money. He would pay her back as soon as he returned to the United States. Over time, the requests increased in frequency and amount, as did business complications preventing him from leaving Dubai. When she had no more funds, Ms. Ziyang begged family members and friends for loans, sending him money via wire transfer. She hoped to help him return to the U.S. quickly, so they could finally spend time together.

Morucci also asked her to open bank accounts for him using her real estate business name, Laughing Waters. Businesses preferred to pay him using U.S. bank accounts. While stuck in Dubai, he could be paid as a consultant for sales referrals. The income would help him refund her money sooner. Morucci instructed her to create a Laughing Waters account in an app called Zoominfo. The service sold access to a database of people and companies used by sales, marketing and recruiting professionals. Ms. Ziyang did as he requested.

Portions of their email and text exchanges were projected on a screen. Morucci's texts were short, rushed. He begged her to trust him, admonishing her when she expressed doubts. He bullied her into quickly responding to his crises before she could think them through logically. If she questioned when they would meet in person, he reassured her they would be together soon. He wanted that, as much or more than she did. Morucci communicated frequently, ending each day and opening each morning with a greeting text, intimating she was always on his mind.

The prosecutor believed she might initially have been a victim. But when the banks and police told Ms. Ziyang she was being scammed, she helped Mr. Morucci anyway. Not only did she use her own funds, but eventually she helped him take money from others.

The Scammer

Mr. Fitch methodically detailed how the crime unfolded: "Morucci is a romance scammer. Scammers use internet dating websites to target vulnerable people, create fake profiles, profess strong feelings soon after connecting with their potential victim, and manufacture a sad story about an urgent need for financial help. While making excuses for delaying an in-person meeting, the scammer asks the victim for money in ever increasing amounts."

Mr. Fitch reported that romance scammers typically originate from Nigeria. I wondered, *Why Nigeria? What was Morucci's story? What did he imagine himself becoming when he was a child? What circumstances led him into crime?* As I contemplated this, it occurred to me that Morucci could have just as easily been a woman.

The Witnesses

The first witness, Mr. Milan Radosevich, was called. Mr.

Radosevich sold his home in Wisconsin to purchase a house in Minnesota to be closer to his grandchildren. Working with a title company, he used the proceeds from the Wisconsin sale to pay over $200,000 for a new house in Eagan, a commuter suburb of the Twin Cities. Before his scheduled closing, Mr. Radosevich emailed the title company to confirm the date and time. He received a confirmation about where to wire his mortgage funds. Mr. Radosevich didn't realize the email was fraudulent, and wired his money as instructed to an account called Laughing Waters, Inc.

A copy of that email was projected for us to view. It looked like a typical business email. When Mr. Radosevich showed up for the closing, the title company representative said she never received his funds, nor heard of Laughing Waters. She denied sending the email. That is when the investigation led to Ms. Ziyang. Mr. Radosevich's money had been deposited into one of the bank accounts set up by Ms. Ziyang for Morucci's referral income.

Mr. Radosevich testified that he and his spouse had another home in Arizona for rental income, where they planned to retire. After their money was stolen, they had to get a temporary mortgage to purchase the Eagan house, so they sold the Arizona home. Three years later, they still pursued legal action against the title company for negligence, trying to get their stolen funds back. I felt anguished about their lost income and dashed hopes for a worry-free retirement.

The defense attorney on cross said he didn't dispute the facts of what happened with Mr. Radosevich's money, but believed Ms. Ziyang was a victim, and her heart got in the way of doing the right thing. She wasn't someone who needed to engage in a scam for money. Her business was quite successful. She was not taking a cut of the money that Morucci got through these scams. *Was that true? How do we know? Will that be proven to us before the trial is over?*

An investigating officer from Santa Clara, California, Lt. Lev Killian, was called as the next witness. He interviewed Ms. Ziyang at her home to ask about the business account where Mr. Radosevich's funds were transferred. When Lt. Killian arrived at her house, Ms. Ziyang delayed speaking to him initially because she was meeting with clients. She agreed to meet the next day instead.

After Killian left, she texted Morucci that the police had visited and asked how to respond. Morucci replied saying she had done nothing wrong. "You cannot be convicted of a crime for not knowing what happened to the funds once you opened those accounts for me. Tell the police you are a victim and followed my instructions." I got goosebumps. *Was Morucci coaching her to build her defense?*

Through the IFP address on Morucci's emails, Lt. Killian confirmed Nigeria as the origin. Mr. Vaurin asked the Lieutenant, "In your many investigations of romance scams, is it typical for the victim not to believe they are part of a scam, even when evidence is provided?"

Lt. Killian responded, "Yes, people are very emotionally upset, crying, and it often takes them a long time to believe the proof. They must be shown by the evidence that there is no doubt."

Mr. Vaurin replied, "Even when they have never met the scammer in person?"

"Not even then."

I looked at Ms. Ziyang frequently. I kept trying to read her facial expression and body language. She only sat quietly. However, when Lt. Killian finished his testimony, Ms. Ziyang solemnly bowed her head toward him with her hands folded together. Evidently, she felt his testimony helped her case. I was not sure. *She looks like a victim but not entirely innocent.*

The next witness, Kelly Partridge, was the closer from the title company who worked with Mr. Radosevich. Despite her name being included in the email, she denied it came from her and had no idea where it had originated. She had no connection with Laughing Waters. I thought, *I'm frightened. How did Morucci access the title company's information about Mr. Radosevich and send an email from that business?* This was not addressed in testimony, but I later learned that it was a specific kind of email fraud. Clearly, the scammer had targets in many places.

We remained on the 13th floor during breaks, standing, stretching, checking our phones, and waiting. The view of the Mississippi River from a window was obscured by frost on the glass, and a fierce wind howled outside. I felt chilled. At 4:40 p.m. we were finally released. I was achy from sitting all day. The insidiousness of this crime depressed me.

I started to wonder exactly when Ms. Ziyang might have questioned the wisdom of her actions. *How could she give up her own hard-earned funds to a man she'd never met? How did she not recognize it was strange to set up different bank accounts using her business name, especially in other states, when bankers and police were telling her it was a scam?*

I felt so very grateful that Andrea and I have a long-term, loving and trusting relationship. When she picked me up, she could tell I was feeling sad and asked how it went. Since I couldn't say anything about the trial, I just replied we were fortunate to have each other. The frigid cold bit at my bones, and I was happy to return to our warm home.

Thursday, January 31

The morning was bitterly icy when Andrea dropped me off. Just before entering the courtroom, I got a text from her.

"I got rear-ended at a stoplight."

"Are you hurt?"

"OK. My neck is stiff. Traffic cops here."

"Oh no. How bad is the car?"

"Dented but drivable."

"I have to go now. Keep me posted."

I felt distracted. After the jury was seated, Mr. Fitch called his first witness whose troubled story unfolded. Mr. Fort wore a plaid suit, had a balding scalp, and sounded like a smoker. He retired from the Minnesota Historical Society where he photographed archival materials on microfiche.

He explained, "In 2014 I fell ill, had a couple surgeries, and then was told by my doctor 'to start living.'" Mr. Fort was single and took care of his sick mother until she died.

He continued, "When my doctor said start living, to me that meant dating. I began using the dating site Match. Within a couple of weeks, I became interested in a woman named Trudy Dale. She sent me her picture." Mr. Fitch showed us Trudy's profile picture. The photo was of a woman who appeared twenty years younger than Mr. Fort. He had a spark in his eyes when he talked about Trudy. More than once Mr. Fort told us she was "very attractive." He was still infatuated.

Mr. Fort and Trudy became acquainted online, and he held out hope of their "starting something together" when she returned to the U.S. On one of his wire transfers to Trudy, the stated purpose was "to help his fiancé." *They had not even met in person, and he presumed marriage?* His funds went to a Laughing Waters account. Trudy told him she was going to Dubai to attend a precious gem conference. Once she arrived, she ran out of money, overspending on her purchases. From that point forward, her requests for financial help continued.

Mr. Fort ended up wiring $98,000 before the investigator contacted him, and Fort realized he was being scammed.

His gullibility, and the amount of cash, shocked me. Perhaps he received an inheritance after his mother passed away. *How can people be so desperate for love and intimacy that they would pay large sums of money to someone they had not even met? How can anyone think a relationship is built this way?*

We broke for lunch. I slipped into Sakura, a sushi restaurant, trying to let go of the stress I was holding. Releasing an audible sigh, I sent Andrea a text.

"How are u feeling?"

"Headache. Arranging repair and rental car."

"I suggest chiro appt."

"Will see how I feel after napping."

"Take care. Love you."

I relaxed a bit before a drawn-out afternoon unfolded in court. The next witness was a lieutenant in economic fraud, Special Agent Thomas Bold. Mr. Bold was hired to investigate the Radosevich wire transfer to Laughing Waters. Bold contacted Lt. Killian in California and asked him to speak to Ms. Ziyang. He also spoke to Mr. Fort, the second victim.

Fitch asked Special Agent Killian, "Did Mr. Fort believe he was the victim of a scam?"

Killian responded with confidence, "Not until he was shown irrefutable evidence. He then agreed to work with the police to get information from Trudy. As soon as he asked pointed questions and stopped sending funds, Trudy disappeared."

Mr. Fort's response was very different from Ms. Ziyang's. She was shown credible evidence of a scam by police and banks, yet she remained loyal to Morucci. Mr. Fort struck me as emotionally immature and less professionally savvy than Ms.

Ziyang. She ran a successful real estate business and was college educated, yet he managed to accept much more quickly that he was the victim of a scam and decided to work with the police to target the scammer. At that moment, Ms. Ziyang no longer appeared innocent to me.

Mr. Fitch inquired, "Once Morucci's internet account was identified as originating from Nigeria, were you able to find and arrest him?"

Bold said, "No, we just turned the evidence over to Nigerian authorities to let them bring the criminal to justice. Typically, they are not successful."

I felt some empathy for Ms. Ziyang. She was getting prosecuted and would likely lose her real estate license. The original perpetrator would just move on to his next victim.

Mr. Fitch held up a pile of paper, representing more than forty exhibits documenting wire transfers and money laundering in accounts set up by Ms. Ziyang on behalf of Morucci, as well as their emails and texts. A self-employed, successful, female immigrant was significantly in debt for money she loaned Morucci, while assisting him in defrauding Mr. Radosevich and Mr. Fort. Her actions struck me as illogical.

The judge anticipated the trial would be completed the next day and released us. I was glad. This trial was a rollercoaster of lies and fraud. Who were the real villains and victims?

Andrea pulled up in front of the courthouse in our Subaru with a dented rear bumper.

"How is the trial going?" she asked.

"It is hard, but they anticipate we will finish tomorrow," I said.

We both felt vulnerable in the world and went to bed early.

Friday, February 1

It was warmer than it had been all week. A high of sixteen was anticipated. This hike in temperature made it a bit easier to face the day.

Mr. Fitch called Ms. Ziyang's brother, Peizhi Ziyang, who had arrived in Minnesota a couple of days prior. He sat in the witness chair, and a female Mandarin Chinese interpreter named Bai Wu stood next to him. They took the oath to tell the truth. Mr. Fitch asked Mr. Ziyang to tell us about the travel boat company he managed.

Through the interpreter Bai Wu, Mr. Ziyang said that his company took tourists on boat cruises down the Yangtze River in China. Mr. Fitch asked about the money he loaned his sister. "Did she say what the loan was for?"

After an exchange in Chinese, the interpreter said, "She told him it was for her 'beautiful man' who had some business trouble."

Fitch asked, "Had his sister asked him for a loan before?"

The interpreter spoke to Mr. Ziyang, then said, "No, never."

Fitch asked, "Does he trust his sister?"

Addressing Ziyang, the interpreter asked, listened, then nodded. "Yes, she is very trustworthy. He is proud of her and her accomplishments. She would not ask for money unless she really needed it."

Fitch asked, "Do you feel your sister is honest?"

I was appalled by these questions of trust and honesty which seemed very subjective and had a hostile undertone. As the interpreter repeated Fitch's question, Peizhi Ziyang knitted his brows together, then spoke. The interpreter replied, "Very honest."

Fitch asked, "Did you have any reason to believe she would not pay you back?"

Mr. Ziyang answered the interpreter quickly. "No, I knew she would."

"Did you have any trouble getting the money together?" asked Fitch.

Mr. Ziyang responded, "I asked my friends to help me get the money together quickly. They gave me a loan because she is my family and needed it."

Fitch asked, "Would it surprise you to learn your sister told several banks she was sending money overseas for a family emergency rather than to help Mr. Morucci with his business?" Listening to the translator, Mr. Ziyang got a confused look on his face and did not respond at first. He glanced at his sister. She looked down. My heart leaped out to him.

Without waiting for an answer, Fitch asked, "Was there a family emergency that required funds to be wire transferred from Ms. Ziyang?"

The interpreter spoke to Mr. Ziyang, then said, "Mr. Ziyang says no." Mr. Fitch said Mr. Ziyang's sister lied to several banks about the purpose of the wire transfers. Those banks included East West, Chase, Bank of America, and Wells Fargo.

Fitch asked, "Do you still think your sister is trustworthy?"

As the interpreter translated, I watched Peizhi Ziyang's face turn from confusion to shock. He looked at his sister, spoke haltingly, and the interpreter said, "Mr. Ziyang cannot respond; he does not know the details."

I looked at Ms. Ziyang, who was obviously distressed. My heart hurt for both of them. *She has lost her family's good will and trust forever.* I felt angry that she involved her brother in the mess she created. Mr. Vaurin had no questions, so Mr. Ziyang was dismissed.

The next witness was Qing Wang, from Sichuan Province in China, along with her Chinese interpreter Zhen Xuan. Fitch asked Ms. Wang to tell us about herself through the interpreter. Ms. Wang was a fifty-two-year-old woman, and Ms. Ziyang's childhood friend. They went to grade school together and remained in touch over the years. She admired and trusted her dear friend Ms. Ziyang and wanted to help her get Morucci back to the U.S. But Ms. Wang did not have enough money to loan Ms. Ziyang, so she mortgaged her house to get funds.

When she explained this, I felt outraged and a little sick to my stomach. I looked at Ms. Ziyang. *How could you do this? I would never ask a friend to mortgage her home and send me money for a virtual romance partner. Even if there was a kernel of truth to his need, it was not a matter of life and death. How could you risk meaningful, lifelong relationships for him?* Perhaps there is a different sense of friendship, family, or loyalty in Chinese culture that I wasn't quite grasping. How could they do these things for Ms. Ziyang without question?

Before we left for lunch, the judge confirmed we would probably finish the trial that day. I was surprised and relieved. I felt stuck in a parallel universe where unusually large sums of money were moved around in an impetuous manner. People mistook virtual connections for love and lied about their intentions.

Upon return, we heard closing arguments. Fitch suggested we read all the evidence provided. Mr. Vaurin reiterated that Ms. Ziyang was a victim, tricked into believing Morucci despite contrary evidence. Her behavior was typical of romance scam victims.

The judge identified two jury alternates who would be dismissed before we deliberated. My friend Brandon was one of them. I felt glad I wasn't an alternate. I was too emotionally invested not to vote for or know the final decision.

Our first task was to identify a foreperson. The judge instructed us, "It is your job to determine if the defendant 'knew or had reason to know' she aided and abetted theft by swindle and received stolen property. You are charged with deciding her innocence or guilt, but if you determine her to be guilty of a felony, I will be responsible for her sentence. After your verdict, I will debrief with you."

For the first time, our cell phones were taken from us. I quickly sent Andrea a text letting her know I had to go offline. I promised to call when I was released, then handed my phone to the deputy sheriff. We were escorted into a conference room just outside the courtroom. The sheriff walked out, shutting the door behind him.

Without stating the reason, one juror suggested a tall, friendly black man be the foreperson. I knew very little about him, except for overhearing his conversations during breaks. He joked in an affable way, worked in the medical field, and seemed intelligent. When no one else volunteered, he accepted the role and notified the sheriff. The foreperson was given a large stack of paper, clipped in sections. This was evidence presented at trial, and there was only one copy, sorted by date. The sheriff left the room again.

We sat in a circle around the large conference table, not sure what to do next. Someone suggested we each say our initial vote. I started. "I vote guilty. The judge's words, 'had reason to know' helped me make my decision. It was subjective if and when she may have known she was aiding and abetting, but police and banks informed her she was being scammed. She had good 'reason to know' and ignored it."

A couple of people wanted to review the correspondence in detail before deciding. It was hard with only one copy of so much paper. I offered to read sections aloud, addressing questions. A female juror strongly felt Ms. Ziyang was a victim and got swept up. She wanted to look closely at the materials herself.

After a relatively short time, we voted again. All agreed Ms. Ziyang was guilty. None of us felt good about our decision on an emotional level, though. I looked at my watch. It had taken about an hour to reach a conclusion. The foreperson notified the sheriff we were ready.

The Verdict

The foreperson signed a form confirming our decision, and then the sheriff escorted us into the courtroom. I didn't look at Ms. Ziyang. The foreperson stated the verdict aloud: "Guilty."

Ms. Ziyang immediately put her head down and started sobbing. From that point forward, when the judge addressed her, she nodded her head yes or no and continued crying, holding her head on crossed arms. I didn't like thinking about what might come next in her life.

The judge dismissed the jury and said to wait for a debrief in the conference room. We sat quietly as the air was thick with our decision. The sheriff handed back our cell phones.

The judge walked in and said in a somewhat joking tone, "My chamber is next door, and I didn't hear any fighting or screaming while you were deliberating, like I sometimes do."

The foreperson said solemnly, "This group was very respectful, and listened to each person's viewpoint before reaching a decision. But that doesn't seem comforting right now." The judge asked us to describe how we were feeling, and almost in unison, we said "awful," "it was hard," "sad," "bad."

The judge told us, "You made the right decision." I was surprised. He asked, "Would it make you feel better to know she continued these behaviors even after arrest for this trial? She is on trial again in the next couple months for the same thing." *Wow.* I asked what her sentence might be. "Because she had no criminal history before this, she might get community service, but if convicted in the second case, her sentence will be more severe."

I asked, "Will her real estate license be terminated?"

"Yes."

Not only did she now have a criminal record, but her means of making a living would be taken. After thanking the judge for his guidance, we each shook his hand and quickly gathered our things. Goodbyes were said as we departed from the elevator. It felt strange to go through something so intense together, knowing I was unlikely to see the others again. I called Andrea to pick me up. Then I bundled into my winter layers and stepped into the cold night air.

Happy to be free.

Epilogue

In the months following the trial, I was curious about Ms. Ziyang's penalty. Ramsey County website lists a "Register of Actions" by case number. I looked up her trial. She was convicted of a felony on both counts. In March she was confined for one day at the Ramsey County prison, then given five years of supervised probation. The total of her combined fees owed was $232,094.47.

Conditions of her probation included the following:

- following laws
- contacting her probation officer
- cooperating with any searches
- giving a DNA sample when directed
- not using or possessing a firearm, ammunition, or explosives
- not registering to vote or voting
- full financial disclosure

- and full access to financial records.

She was also assigned 100 hours of community service, each hour to be approved by her probation officer. Though the past winter had been long and harsh, Ms. Li Mei Ziyang's future looked even bleaker.

SHATTERED

CHRISTINA HOAG

I knew early on in my relationship with James that something was off about him. There were the annoying, small things. He cut in lines, angering people, and embarrassing me. He raided my son's Lunchable boxes for the candy. He lost his keys and demanded I leave work to help him look for them. Then, there were the more sinister things. He told me he had mysterious contacts at my job who were keeping tabs on me. He stood at the front door literally blocking me from seeing my neighbor. He hunted through my email, trash included, when I left my computer on.

But James would also do things like take me on a weekend trip to a resort where he wrapped me up in towels on a cold beach, fetched me drinks and soaped my back in hot bath of scented water. He hired me a cleaning lady. He bought me evening clothes and squired me around chic restaurants and clubs. Perhaps most importantly, he told me over and over that I was an uber-talented writer who just needed a lucky break, that people had underestimated me my whole life, that I deserved more.

So, I dismissed the negative things as quirks and reasoned they made him exciting and dramatic. I rationalized there had be a downside to the upside. To get the highs, I had to put up with the lows.

In fact, these behaviors, both good and bad, were hallmarks of an abusive relationship, signposts pointing the way to impending disaster. I didn't *realize* that at the time, but deep down I *knew* it. I simply refused to acknowledge my gut instinct because I wanted the relationship so badly.

I met James when I was a newspaper reporter in Miami, a forty-three-year-old single mom and former foreign correspondent. One morning, a man called the newsroom saying he had a story about the South Florida mob. Intrigued, I went to meet him. In the middle of our conversation, he asked me out to dinner. Taken aback, I turned him down, saying it was a conflict of interest since he was a source. I didn't even know if I liked him. He was loud and brash, yet possessed a genuineness, a rough-hewn charm.

My editors decided James's story idea wasn't worth pursuing, but over the next six months, he'd check in with me from Los Angeles, where he lived although he travelled frequently to Florida.

After a long phone conversation with him one day, I realized I liked him. He seemed genuinely interested in me, and his attention was flattering. On his next trip to Florida, I accepted his dinner invitation.

It was a magical evening. As the sky turned into a palette of oranges and pinks, we sat at a bayfront restaurant. A balmy breeze caressed my back. Yachts clinked against their moorings with the gentle tide. As I sipped a glass of Chablis, James leaned his head on an arm, smiled and said, "Tell me everything about you." A warm glow spread inside me. As night dropped around us like a cocoon, I told him about my childhood growing up around the world, my adventurous career.

"Christina," James said when I finished, "you're the most interesting person I have ever met." I slipped right into his smile like taking a long drink of water.

Less than two weeks later, he told me he was in love with me. He'd jump on a plane to be with me. He'd call me at all hours of the day or night just to hear my voice. It was a movie romance come true.

"You're the best thing that's ever happened to me," James said. "No one sees you like I do, Christina. I see the real you."

And I truly felt he did. "You're an angel sent to me from heaven," I told him and meant it.

The first serious incident occurred one night we were at a casino with his friends. I was talking to one of the guys when James demanded I fetch him a glass of water. Annoyed at both his interruption and tone, I didn't respond, and he stormed off. An hour later, he returned and called me an asshole in front of everyone. I wanted to leave, but I was stuck. James had driven. On the way home, he pulled off the highway and apologized. He refused to drive until I accepted his apology. So, I did.

That should've been the end of it, but it wasn't. After six years of few dates with no one I found the slightest bit interesting, I craved a real relationship. I overlooked the incident as an aberration.

After a few months, he asked me to move to LA, but I wasn't keen to uproot my life. He ramped up the pressure. "Miami's a backwater. You can't maximize your talent here," he said. "Besides, you're getting old, opportunities are going to dry up. Just come and check it out." So, I did.

One night he pulled a Jekyll-and-Hyde. He went into a gas station and returned in a frightening rage, accusing me of having sex in the back of a restaurant with a waiter, calling me a scumbag. When we arrived at his apartment, I packed my bag, ready to get to the airport and leave on the first flight to anywhere. He grabbed my wrist and threw me. Luckily, I landed on the bed. I got up warily, shocked, and scared. He immediately apologized.

"It'll never happen again," he said. "I'm just insecure. I'm bad at relationships. I don't want to lose you. You don't want to lose me, do you?" He kept talking as I walked down the hall with my roller bag. When I reached the front door, he darted in front of me blocking my exit. "You don't want to throw away everything we have together, do you?"

His arrow hit home. The truth was, I didn't want to throw it away. I really wanted a place in the coveted Kingdom of Coupledom. I ended up caving on everything. I quit my job, sold my house, and moved.

Once I was far from family and friends, James's erratic behavior escalated as his worship of me evaporated. He stranded me at the beach, accused me of having sex with random men, checked up wherever I was going, hovered over me as I made phone calls. Every day was an ordeal that centered around not triggering James. My son hated him. Fortunately, James largely ignored him.

I could no longer dismiss the gut feeling that had warned me at the start of the relationship. Something was drastically wrong with James and in moments of clarity, he acknowledged it.

"You don't know what it's like to be me," he said. "I have this huge black hole inside me."

That was enough to give me a thread of hope, just long and thick enough for me to counter my gut feeling and continue in the relationship. Now my reasoning went, if he could get therapy and mood-stabilizing meds, our relationship would be perfect.

Despite his numerous promises to seek therapy, he never did. In the meantime, I felt myself crumble and another person appear. This woman lied, sneaked, and manipulated to do things like get her mail without James inspecting it, attended school events without his jealous fits, summoned tears so he'd end his tirades sooner.

It was me who ended up seeking a therapist.

"Christina, you're in an abusive relationship and you have to leave," she told me as I sobbed on her couch. "But it will probably be the most difficult thing you've ever done."

One morning a few weeks later, I was walking across the living room to the kitchen, and I noticed bits of paper littering the floor like confetti. Puzzled, I picked them up and recognized them—they were photos of me. An icy feeling gripped me, but I had no time to process it. The front door banged open, and James marched in, his face contorted, eyes bulging. He was in one of his terrifying rages.

With his six-foot-three frame towering over me, he jabbed a forefinger in my face. "You're poisoning my pills! I'm taking them to my cop friend and having them tested!"

My gut instinct screamed at me: James was insane—and dangerous. This time, I paid attention. After he left, I called a moving company. That evening, as I sat in a hotel after stowing my stuff in storage and picking up my son, I wondered how I'd got myself into this mess. The warning signs were there from the get-go. Why had I stayed? I felt utterly alone and overwhelmed with shame. But I had to focus on rebuilding my life. I got a job and an apartment.

James, however, hadn't gone away. He'd found out where I was by following me when I picked up my son from school. He begged me to come back. The truth was I missed him, terribly. I yearned for the good James when he chose to show up. So, I went back to him, but the key was I didn't move back in with him. That allowed me the space to wean myself off him, like a drug addict, to regain my strength, to recover my sense of self. When he came into my workplace afterhours and wanted to steal office supplies, I stood up to him and said no. He backed down.

The reunion lasted three months. The breaking point came when my son reported that James had given him $50 to spy on me. I wasn't going to let him manipulate my child, as he had with me. I ended it, but this time I was stronger.

James left me flowers, ambushed me outside my apartment, broke into my building to wax my car and hammer at my door. He showed up at my mother's house in Florida when I was there and on my flight back to LA. He got my records from the phone company to see who I was talking to. He called me at work and had his celebrity friends call me. He called my colleagues, my sister, my friends, saying I was unstable, that he was trying to help me. I changed my phone number. He got my new number. I changed it again. He sent me emails and instant messages. Every time he popped up, I blocked him like in a game of Whack-A-Mole. After months of this, he faded, and I breathed easier.

Exactly a year after the breakup, sheriff's deputies showed up at my workplace with a restraining order filed by James against me. All the harassment he had done to me he declared I had done to him. He even had a letter by a woman swearing under oath that she'd seen scratches on his face that I allegedly inflicted on him. Using my investigative skills, I discovered that the woman had a lengthy criminal record and had been in prison at the time she said she saw the scratches.

I was contacted by new friends of his who said he was obsessed by getting revenge. He wanted to get me fired from my job, have my son taken away, take my savings. They said he'd been evicted from his apartment and was on crystal meth.

I found a domestic violence support group and hired a lawyer. At the court hearing, James bumbled and fumbled in his arguments for granting the restraining order. The judge dismissed his case.

I did not hear from James until ten years later almost to the day. I received two messages via social media from someone purporting to be James's nephew, who said James needed to speak to me as soon as possible and listed a phone number. I deleted the messages. The next day my stepmother received the same message, which she also trashed.

Those messages told me James hadn't changed one iota and never would. The person who'd changed was me. When I read those messages, my legs didn't quake. My stomach didn't churn. I felt no shame or humiliation. James was simply something that happened to me.

While I'd never want to go through that experience again, I owe James an odd debt of gratitude. I'm more confident and secure in myself. Most of all, I learned that my gut feeling is always right. I just have to pay attention to it and heed it. It's not the easiest thing to do, especially when what you want is the exact thing your gut says is bad for you. I have no idea how intuitive gut instinct really works, but it is there for a reason—protection. It truly has your best interests at heart, more than your brain. Your mind can play tricks on you, convince you that it'll be all right, to just go for it. It can override that gut feeling. That's the danger. I assume intuition is centered in some primitive part of our brains, dating back to our cavemen ancestors. But there's a reason we still have it over eons of evolution. It works.

I'VE BEEN SWINDLED

REBECCA RUSH

I once dated a famous librarian I met on Facebook.

When I walked into the dimly lit Cafe Routier in Westbrook, Connecticut, in the fall of 2009, there was a martini in front of J. He told me he'd gotten there early to drink before I arrived. I was living at my Mom's after leaving Miami a year earlier. My Mother hid magnum bottles of Chardonnay in the China cabinet, preferring to drink it warm rather than admit that she was drinking. To avoid her, I went to happy hour after work and pretended I worked late. The only problem I thought I had with drinking was everyone else's reaction to it. Except for J's.

I fell in love with that.

He was so confident that it seemed weird when he undressed the first time we went to bed together, and he was just a normal-looking guy.

The first time J met my friend George, he walked straight up to turn off the flat screen and started fussing with his hair. He was always immaculately dressed, though his apartment was disgusting. Threadbare hand-me-down furniture, rotting food, and piles of clothing draped across every surface. He had a bad tooth and left floss picks everywhere. But he looked great in expensive suits, his hair swooped to the side.

He liked relationships like he liked the bar at a wedding—open—but we were only together a month when he asked me to be exclusive. The idea of an open relationship terrified me, which was insane considering that in every relationship I'd ever been in I'd either cheated or been cheated on. I thought I wanted honesty, but all I knew were secrets.

J traveled a lot for conferences, for the teaching of "new media" to the libraries of the country. Facebook power point presentations, the use of unnecessary abbreviations to prove yr cool, whatever else he did. When he was home, he told me people without enemies have no character and showed me his socks that said, "I heart haters."

He invited me to what he described as a black-tie event in New York City with his family, a benefit for a long-dead cousin. He picked out a strapless black satin ABS gown at Bloomingdales, and I waited for him to pull out his wallet for what felt like an eternity before plunking down my entire paycheck.

We walked into a ballroom that looked like a public-school cafeteria. Several things already in my closet would have been fine. We did have a really good time according to my Instagram. I posted a photo of us kissing. I wanted to be Facebook official. He refused, citing his professional brand as a playboy librarian.

A female friend of his came to visit, and I intuitively knew not to contact him that weekend. I stalked his social media accounts except for that one locked Twitter. "It's mostly for my siblings," he had said.

"Brazilian food with my Brazilian girl," one of his Foursquare check-ins read.

Through my work accounts I came across a group of four

female librarians who said fuck a lot. One followed me back, then unfollowed me immediately. Another followed me first and messaged asking if I knew J.

"Yeah," I replied, "He's my boyfriend." She unfollowed me. One set her account to private. J flew in from a conference that night, and I made him drive through a blizzard to my mother's house. It resolved nothing, but I wanted the action to prove something.

He said the four of them were a group of old, ugly, haters. One of them was psychotically obsessed with him. The others hated him on her behalf. I bought it like a dress that's too small, telling myself it will fit by spring, and then housed two Boston Cream donuts.

He invited me home for Christmas in Upstate New York. His mother's house was huge and modern, floor-to-ceiling windows in the back, revealing a deep-green forest. When we woke in the morning, we'd find coffee made and slip Bailey's into it before I let my dog out. Relaxed and morning-drunk in the hot tub, I brought up the four horsewomen again.

"Maybe we should just break up."

"How am I going to get home then?"

We made up in time for lunch. We were in the middle of nowhere. It was Christmas. Nobody wants to ring in the New Year alone.

After that, J left for a conference in California that he was very excited to attend. I wanted to go. "Next year," he promised.

Every place he went that librarian who was obsessed with him checked in as well. He told me that she waited until he checked in somewhere and then checked in there herself so it would look like they were together.

Our sex life left something to be desired - each other - and we didn't have a lot. Most of the time we did he would wake me up in the middle of the night, turn me over, finish quickly, and fall back asleep. I woke up predawn and snuck into his liquor cabinet, every time hoping the next gulp of vodka or Patron or even gin, which I hated, would help me sleep until I woke up refreshed without a hangover. I let entire days pass that way. We could always make up some excuse to drink together on Sunday - Bellini's and vegan nachos. Bellini's with *pear nectar*. If it's fancy, it isn't alcoholism.

That March, sex was so infrequent it was starting to affect me on an emotional level. I felt more desired by my Twitter followers than my own boyfriend. I told him I needed to take a break, but I didn't like myself enough to fully commit to being alone. Scarcely six weeks went by before I found myself alone, drunk and texting him at karaoke.

"I feel like you don't want me."

"But I do want you. So much."

We went to New Orleans together for the annual library convention. I got drunk on street drinks and spent the evening puking in our hotel room, while he went out to hang with friends. We went to a library event in a World War 2 museum and saw that the obsessed librarian had checked in there as well. We spent the evening staying one exhibit ahead of her.

We also went to his mother's camp in the Thousand Islands that summer, straddling New York State and Canada, the water so deliciously cold and clear I felt cleaner after jumping into it than I ever had in my life.

When we got back, he said we should move to California.

"Do you want to make $11 an hour and live in your mom's house for the rest of your life?"

When my stepfather left, my mother suggested that J move in with us so that we could save to move. She didn't count on him quitting his job at Yale soon after and being around so much. Nobody counted on the pregnancy. Right before we found out, we went to the Turks and Caicos for his thirtieth birthday. I don't know how I didn't know. My tits looked amazing against the Caribbean Sea.

I was as fertile as I was irresponsible, much like I kept drinking over and over expecting it to work out differently. I kept relying on birth control pills that I took a week in or forgetting to take them for days.

I talked to him about keeping it. "I don't want KIDS," he spat.

When I told my mother, she said, "Obviously you can't keep it," and then reminded me that my younger's sister's baby shower was a week away and not to make that about me. I went to the party feeling fat and nauseous and spent the entire time talking about myself.

At a weekend conference I attended with him, I turned to him in bed. "There's life inside of me that's ours." He turned his head, then body, away, and went to sleep. I lay there, my hand on my stomach, staring at the ceiling for hours.

I scheduled an appointment the next day to get the abortion pill. I went back to the doctor to confirm it worked. I scheduled an appointment to get an IUD six weeks later when my vagina was healed. If you don't know what an IUD is, it's a device that they put in your uterus that stops you from writing abortion jokes.

My boobs weren't the only thing that grew that summer. My Twitter followers had reached the thousands from the jokes I'd been writing by following popular formats. My first tweet that did well was, "I call it a rack because I use it to hold things up, like my soda, my Yorkie, and my self-esteem."

"You're acting like a slut on Twitter, talking about your boobs all the time!" J chided.

I found Viagra in his things. He pointed back to the time before our break when we were having a hard time having sex.

"I thought there was something wrong with me," he said. "There isn't." His unspoken words hung in the air like an unborn child.

"Also, your mom keeps trying to get me to talk shit about you?"

I went to a Twitter meetup called Snark NYC for people that were funny on Twitter.

"What do you do?" a woman asked me.

"I'm a Social Media Manager. You?"

"I'm a stand-up comic. I write jokes. Do you write jokes?"

"I guess, kind of...on Twitter."

"You should write a five-minute set and send it to me."

I proceeded to get so drunk that I smoked a bowl in the bar bathroom and got kicked out. In a blackout, I took a cab back to the hotel suite that I was sharing with several Twitter mutuals. I was told they arrived back to the room to see me wandering around naked, alone, shouting, "I'm not that kind of girl!"

I went back to the doctor to get the IUD and found out I was pregnant again. Keeping it wasn't a question this time. Sometimes the trauma of forced miscarriage makes the body drop another egg early. Nobody tells you that. I had the second abortion, and no sex until the ache from my newly inserted IUD wore off. It was almost my thirtieth birthday. There was a restaurant in Boston that I wanted J to take me to.

He followed me into the kitchen one night while I was roasting root vegetables. He said, "Don't put oil and salt on them, you put oil and salt on everything!"

"You think a banana is a fun snack!" I shouted back. "A banana is not a snack! A banana is something you eat on the way to a snack!"

My mother cornered me in her kitchen. "You don't have to let him talk to you this way," she said. "You don't have to take this. He's mean."

Later that evening he walked up behind me. "We can't go to that restaurant you want to go to in Boston for your birthday, I'm sorry."

I turned around. "Why?"

"Because we're going to JAMAICA!"

We left on my birthday.

That morning we waited to check in at the head of a line that faced a bank of airline employees. J waited directly behind someone checking in while I stood at the end of the roped-off line. He was far to the left when someone opened a new station directly to my right and motioned me over. I checked in. "Happy birthday," the gentleman said. I smiled.

J came up fuming. "You cut in front of me!!!"

"Oh my god, dude, you were super far away. We're getting on *the same plane.*"

We didn't speak for the next hour. We arrived in Jamaica, and I bought an ounce of weed from the guy who drove us from the airport. We stopped at a shack for the best Jerk chicken I have ever had. I was stoned more constantly than I could usually afford to be. Even more, for the first time in the year we had been together, J didn't give me any shit about it.

I wanted to take a horseback ride through a banana plantation like we saw in a brochure in the lobby of our hotel. We were eating dinner on the patio when a man came around to the tables offering horseback rides for about $20 less per person than the brochure.

"Through the banana plantation?" I asked.

"Oh, yes, of course miss, through the plantation, of course."

We signed up to go the next day. The man picked us up at our hotel and took us to the place where the smiling people that served tourists lived. Clothing and children swung from the trees. I was sure that when I climbed atop the horse it would collapse. A man had to follow it with a palm switch hitting it on the flank to get it to walk at all, and it stumbled constantly. I hadn't seen ribs that defined since private school. J climbed atop his dying horse looking like a baby trying a lemon. We arrived at the top of a small hill where the guide gestured for us to enjoy the view. It was foggy.

As the horses stumbled down the hill, J and I exchanged worried glances. We weren't going back the way we came.

They led us into a forest and motioned for us to get off our horses. They tied the horses to palm trees and motioned for us to walk down a path strewn with roots and leaves. The words, *I am going to die today,* floated through my brain. At the end of the path was a clearing. Inside the clearing were old tires. Inside the tires were young marijuana plants.

"Take a picture," said my guide. "No thanks," I said.

"No, no, you must take a picture. Is free. Take a picture."

"That's alright."

"It's no cost, take the picture, please, take it."

I took a picture.

"$30."

"You must buy ganja," another said. "Good price," he said. He held a machete. J quivered in a way I'd only seen him do when there was a bug in the house.

"No, thank you, I already bought all the ganja I need, got it from the taxi driver. Too much ganja, thank you, no thank you, no, I don't need any more ganja."

We walked back down the path in silence.

Then, J broke the silence with "I've been swindled!"

We flew home the next day. I let him check in first.

Nearly a year after that woman suggested I try comedy the night I blacked out and became comedy, I went to an open mic. Some people were working toward good, some people sucked, and nobody got murdered when they got off stage. My Twitter friend Stephanie went up for her first time. When her set failed and everyone sat silent and staring, she yelled, "I HAVE A VAGINA!" and pulled her skirt up like I did when I was little and had to go potty.

I was ready to try. I made a Facebook event. I got too drunk and heckled the comics on stage before me. When I got up, my drunk coworkers cheering, I read 27 of my tweets and felt alive.

I broke up with J right before Thanksgiving, which I planned to work through. My mother had long grown sick of him and the fact that he refused to talk shit about me with her.

Two days before Thanksgiving, J was at the house packing to go to his family's for the holiday. When he got back, he was supposed to move out.

Work was super busy that day, everyone wanting to get their Grateful Dead or Big Bang Theory T-Shirt Christmas orders in early. My family was celebrating at the beach that year in the three houses we owned at the end of a dead-end street. Even my cousin, his wife, and their two kids flew in from California.

All morning my mother was texting me about J.

"I WANT HIM OUT OF MY HOUSE!!!"

And I was texting J on her behalf.

"You're leaving today, right?"

And J was texting me about my mother.

"I'm getting ready to go to my parents. Your mother is drunk and crazy."

"Rebecca, HE NEEDS TO GET OUT OF MY HOUSE NOW."

"Your mother is really drunk. I'm scared."

"Can you both just wait until I get home for lunch."

"Mom, he's leaving soon."

"J, this is just what she does."

"Rebecca, you have to come now. Your mother fell down the stairs. I don't know if she's breathing."

"J, this is just what she does. Don't DO ANYTHING. I'll be home for lunch soon."

As soon as I pulled off the main road into the neighborhood, I felt a familiar hole in my gut. As I pulled onto the street I saw the ambulance, the police car, my aunts, my cousins, their children, and their husbands on my mother's front lawn.

J was standing off to the side crying. My mother was on a stretcher. She turned her head when she saw me.

"I only had one drink!"

My oldest cousin, Bobby, pulled me aside.

"So, um, I guess your mother was drunk, and fell down the stairs, and then J called 911. When the cops got here, she told them he pushed her and that he wasn't supposed to be here. They almost arrested him. They took his house keys."

I followed the ambulance to the hospital and went back to work.

J took his Viagra and left. The cops took statements from the rest of my family. They went inside the house and found dozens of empty bottles of Chardonnay in my mother's closets, and an empty blackberry brandy bottle next to the bed.

I got a call from the hospital. My mother was ready to be released. I walked into the Shoreline Medical Center and past the reception without waiting for instructions. I had been there before. I walked through triage and saw my mother. She had no shoes, only hospital socks. Her face brightened.

The nurse addressed us both as the same time as if she were speaking to a small child.

"She's agreed to go to AA," said the nurse. My mother nodded.

AA was where my mother sent *me*. I was the one with the problem. She was a binge drinker. Sure, some of her binges had lasted several years, but not lately. She would stay dry for months at a time every time she did a fad diet. She did all of them. Cabbage soup, Atkins, the cookie diet. Then she'd get a sparkle in her eye and grumble, "I'm going to be badddd" and down an entire gallon of Peppermint ice cream in bed. Next day it would be back to warm Chardonnay hidden in cabinets.

I helped her to her feet, and she grasped my arm, hard.

"I only had one drink," she insisted.

We weren't out the door of the hospital when she said, "The cats! The shrimp! How could they keep me so long! I special-ordered jumbo shrimp for the cats, and the fish market is going to close!"

It was already dark outside.

"Mom, I have to go back to work."

"You're going to take me to Atlantic Fish Market first. I don't know if they're open tomorrow."

I turned the car that way. She handed me her credit card. The store was dark, but I got out of the car and pulled on the glass door anyway. Closed.

"Awwww, goddamit." Having to feed the cats grocery store shrimp was the biggest problem that she had.

I drove her home, dropped her off, and went back to work. When I got home, J was gone. I went upstairs to smoke some weed on the deck off my room. I went down into the kitchen and stared out the window.

Without him I would be stuck with her. Without J, this would be my life. When she came to, she explained it was his fault she drank, and I finally understood what she meant when she told the cops that it was his fault that she had fallen down the stairs. She thought it was because she was mad at him that she drank, and because she drank, she fell down the stairs.

"It wouldn't have happened if HE was gone like he was supposed to be! Also, I have a COLD! That's why I had black-berry brandy, for my cold! I only had a little this morning because it was on my nightstand."

I had been crawling over her body on stairs in homes we lived in for decades now, sometimes dragging her by an ankle to her room if her room was on the same floor as the one she passed out on.

My Twitter friend Stephanie, the one who had flashed the crowd trying stand up, told me, "You don't have to choose between your mom or some guy. You can do this life thing on your own."

Maybe that was true for her.

I texted J.

"I don't want to break up. Can I come to your family's for Thanksgiving?"

I left the next day after work, despite the fact that it was more important for me to be at work on Black Friday than any other day of the calendar year.

I arrived around 11 pm, relieved at having put six hours of distance between me and my mother. I slipped into the warm blanket of his family. I smoked cigarettes with his mother. I smoked pot and talked about comedy at a different house with his father. I ate and drank and smoked and pretended nothing bad had happened, just like I'd been taught.

J stayed with his mom for a while we figured out what to do. Mine had decided that it was time for me to move out: "You've been here two years. It's enough. I'm enabling you. You can't stay forever. "

J and I found a realtor, and a hotel he could stay at near my mom's house until we signed a lease. He wanted me to stay with him, and when I refused, preferring to stay in my own, free room, he tried to make me pay for half of the hotel anyway.

"Nice try," I told him. "I'm not the one who pushed my mom down the stairs then called the cops."

We found a house in Old Saybrook, a winter rental nobody yet had taken. It was more than we planned on spending, but it was right near the water, furnished, and most importantly, they would give it to us. J didn't want me to smoke weed in the house at all, but we compromised on the bathroom.

My daily routine that Christmas season was work at least ten hours, come home, sit in the driveway, and smoke a cigarette. Breeze by J, who would be sitting in the living room like a puppy or a 1930's housewife, say hi to the dog, and lock myself in the bathroom in the hall.

If met with too much resistance on my way to the bathroom, I would say, "Long day at work, gotta smoke real quick."

Once locked in the bathroom I would pack up my one hitter, light it, and smoke. I would stick my left hand in my pants and masturbate. I would smoke, and I would masturbate. I masturbated and I smoked. I stood facing the mirror but not looking at myself.

When J wasn't home sitting on the couch, he was either at a conference or working from a tea shop nearby preparing for his next conference. He had a flirtation with a girl who worked at the tea shop, but it failed to get my attention, no matter how much he told me about it.

Years later, I found a conversation between us that had been uploaded via iMessage and saved to my iPad:

"Hey, how about a blowjob tonight."

"So, I used my Dad's Amazon gift certificate to get stuff for the house! Toothpaste, paper towels, toilet paper. This is so awesome that you can buy that stuff on Amazon now."

"Hmm, how about that blowjob."

"Oh, I also got laundry detergent!!!"

Soon New Year's Eve was upon us, and nobody in my office had made plans. We had been too busy trying to get through each day. Online shopping was really taking off that year, and we had a lot of licensed items that nobody else had. On a good day, you might feel like one of Santa's elves. On a bad day, you might feel like one of Santa's elves from David Sedaris' *Santa-Land Diaries*.

"We'll throw a party at my house!" I offered.

J wasn't into it, and I didn't care.

All of the customer service department came. Stephanie arrived with a young date and Adderall, Xanax, and an enormous bottle of Grey Goose. My new hire, Elisha, came with her boyfriend.

The rest of the call center arrived bearing booze, along with some of the warehouse workers. At J's insistence that pot not be smoked openly, I sectioned off the second bedroom as the pot smoking area. I was in there a lot, laughing with my friends. It began to snow, adding to the accumulated feet already on the ground. J got deep into a bottle of tequila, standing in the kitchen with a girl from the warehouse, as they passed the bottle back and forth and discussed how being a vegan made them far superior to meat eaters.

I found him holding the empty bottle. "J, maybe you should slow down."

"Stephanie's boyfriend drank all this!" He offered, "But it's okay. They brought that huge bottle of Grey Goose, and it's on top of the fridge. I did the math!"

I went back into the second bedroom to smoke a blunt someone had rolled up. J started knocking on the door.

"I know you're doing cocaine in there! I hope you're enjoying your cocaine!"

Soon after, he called me into the tiny kitchen. Once I was in there, he grabbed my hair. Hard.

"You never listen," he growled.

I shook it off and smoked more weed. Afterwards, I stepped onto the deck into the falling snow. It was near midnight, and half the party was out there smoking cigarettes. I lit one.

"So, like I was saying," J said to my coworkers, "I haven't had sex with a Brazilian girl in four months!"

"We've been together 16 months. You mean that you haven't had sex with a Brazilian girl in at least 16 months."

"I haven't had sex with a Brazilian girl in four months!!!"

And that was how I found out, through doing the math, that he cheated on me.

The clock struck midnight. People cheered. I went back inside and stood in the kitchen. J approached me.

"I need to call my sister. You changed the passcode on my phone. I need to call my sister." He waved the phone in my face. He grabbed my hair again. "You never listen!!"

Elisha's boyfriend Bill, a bear of a man, saw him. "I think that's enough for you, buddy," he said. "Time for you to take a nap." He picked him up and flung him over his shoulder like a sack of toys. He carried him to the master bedroom, depositing him on the bed like gifts nobody wanted.

He stayed in there a few minutes, and then came back out, gunning for me.

"You locked my phone! I need to call my sister! I hate you! You're a crazy bitch! Let me into my phone! Give me my car keys!"

He grabbed my hair for the last time. I insisted, "I don't really care about what happens to you right now, but I'll be damned if I give you your keys and you hit some innocent person, or a car with kids in it."

Bill picked him up again, carried him back to the bedroom.

I went back outside. Lit another cigarette. Looked up at the stars, the falling snow. A new year. 2012.

My coworker Kelly, the kind of girl who would come back from the bathroom at work and plop down at her desk, announcing, "My pussy stinks!" and always told customers to mail their returns in vanilla envelopes, pushed open the deck door.

"Becca. J is crawling down the street with his iPad tucked between his chin and his chest."

I finished my smoke and checked his Facebook. There it was.

A new post.

PLease. Help. Me. My crazy ex girlfriend is holding me host stage.

Next thing I knew the police were at my door. His sister had seen the post and messaged him. He had his iPad because he had locked himself out of his phone with his drunk-ass fingers. She called the police in Westchester, who called the police in Old Saybrook. The police arrived, investigating the claims that we were holding him hostage and doing cocaine. The house stunk like weed. The police asked everyone to stay until they were done with their questioning. Stephanie rose, pressed a handful of Xanax into my hand, and left. An officer walked down the hallway to the bedroom. "Hey!" He called back to his partner. "This only locks from the inside! He said they locked him in the bedroom."

I explained I took his keys because he was drunk. That he locked himself out of his phone. Bill, and every other person at the party, brought up the fact that he assaulted me three times.

"It's a pretty wild claim that you all are holding him hostage," one said, "considering he's not even here."

During the questioning, the vegan girl from the warehouse who had shared the bottle of tequila had a full, moaning, orgasm in her sleep on the couch she was passed out on, in front of everyone.

The cops left to look for J and found him in a nature reserve down the street from our house. They arrested him for assault and cuffed him there.

I watched the scene unfold from far away, like from another planet, the way I had watched myself move through most of my life. Like it was somebody else's.

Then his mother called, shouting into the phone, trying to verbally strong arm me into undoing something I hadn't done. Was it my fault? On some level, sure. In a way, I was holding J hostage because I didn't want to live with my mother anymore and didn't see a way I could afford a place on my own for me and my dog.

This swirled in my head along with the wine and Xanax and pot as I tried to formulate a response.

"Melanie. I didn't call the cops. Your son called the cops. I didn't tell them that he assaulted me. Everyone at the party that bore witness to it told them he assaulted me. I didn't press charges. The cops pressed charges. There is nothing I can do for you, and I don't know anything else. I am going to go now."

Once the cops hauled him to jail, everyone left, one by one. Then I was worse than alone.

I sat on the couch and held my little dog, rocking and crying. I looked up and spotted the bottles on top of the fridge. Everyone left their liquor behind. I broke into a bottle of red, and, finishing it, began on the large bottle of Grey Goose. There was an acid facial peel that I had ordered from China on Amazon that I hadn't tried yet. I pulled out the instructions. It called for baking soda to neutralize the acid after you had left it on a maximum of 5-8 minutes. I didn't have baking soda, and the print on the thin piece of paper swam in front of my eyes. Drinking directly from the Grey Goose bottle, I covered my face in acid.

I slapped on extra around my chin area, where I had had clogged pores, acne, and the subsequent scars. I left it on at least a half an hour, maybe a full hour. I kept drinking the vodka. I smoked pot openly in every area of the house. When I finally went to the sink to wash my face, the stinging didn't stop. Chunks of my face came off. Adding soap made it worse. My entire face was raw and red, but around my mouth and chin, I looked like I was wearing a beard of third-degree burns. I could barely open my mouth to cry or drink. This was how I spent New Year's Day, 2012. I called out of work the next day and continued to work on the bottle. Chunks of my face continued to fall off. Drunk in bed, I picked at the scabs as they formed, sometimes stopping when I withdrew fingers covered in blood.

A comic I had met a few times came over. He was someone I never would have had sex with. I don't remember much of his visit other than him turning me around on the couch so he could shove himself inside me without looking at my burnt-off face. I don't remember if he used a condom, I don't remember what he said or when he left. I don't remember anything until days later.

I was still sitting on the couch when I saw J inserting his key into the door on the back deck.

He entered. "I didn't think you would be here! You're supposed to be at work!" I had packed up all his things as he had instructed me to, even the Christmas presents I had bought him late that hadn't arrived by New Years. I held back a few whiskey rocks to throw in the ocean later.

"Who else did you cheat on me with?" I asked.

"There was this woman, at a conference, she came on to me, she reached for my dick. It got hard..."

I shook my head.

He pointed at a spot on the couch to my right.

"You had sex!" he said. "There's cum on the couch! You cheated ON ME!"

I stared straight ahead like a patient in a 50's mental ward right after electroshock therapy.

"I'm sorry about your face," he said, walking out the door with his presents.

I sliced open a t-shirt his mother had bought me that said 'Love' in cursive in the middle of a heart. I cut the love open. I left the knife next to it. Then I positioned all the social media magnets I had gotten him for Christmas but hadn't told him about around the hole where the love was missing, so that I could feel okay about keeping them.

Dislike. Thumbs Down. Unfriend. I posted this scene on Instagram.

Later that day the phone rang. It was the Brazilian girl who was also one of the dirty librarian chicks on Twitter. It was also the friend from Florida who had visited J right after he asked me to be exclusive. It was the psycho who stalked him in California and checked in places after him. We stayed on the phone for hours. She and J were dating when I met him. Because it was long distance, she dealt with the open relationship that he wanted. She knew about me. That was what all the check-ins at the California conference were about.

Propped up by the faith of a stranger in Florida and the resilience you find when you break all the way to the bottom, I returned to work. My face began to heal. I cried and drove a long way along the shoreline playing Gotye. I stopped and threw things into the ocean that reminded me of him, one by one, starting with the whiskey rocks.

Then I started regularly going to open mics to drink whiskey and talk shit about J. Once when a host saw me approaching the stage he said, "Here comes Rebecca to talk about how much she hates MEN!" But I kept going, and I kept thinking of things to talk about - how other people had wronged me, mostly. One day I was on stage in Rhode Island, and I forgot my set. I looked out at the crowd and started talking about how my sister blocked me on Facebook, how I thought I was the first Jew on food stamps, how awkward it was to pull the card out of my Louis Vuitton wallet. Someone in the crowd shouted, "What are you doing later?" And I shot back, "Not you." I became myself up there, before I even knew who that was. When I left, I felt different than I had ever felt in my life. I didn't need J. I didn't need my mother. I didn't need anyone to tell me how good my set was. I didn't need - anyone. I found a high worth chasing.

That was how I threw myself into stand-up comedy. How I threw myself all the way in.

A FOREIGN TASTE

LISA MONTAGNE

This is my first confession: I *love* food. I am on a constant quest for that perfect bite—a balance of sweet, salt, acid, and crunch washed down with the perfect swallow of dry Champagne. I would marry food if I could. That's how much I love it. Obviously, I didn't marry food, but here's another confession: When I was eighteen years old, I married an Englishman. He liked the look of me; I liked his accent. My parents were distracted by their divorce. But at eighteen what did I know about anything? At nineteen, I got knocked up after an episode with a broken condom on the 4th of July. I'm sure there's some joke here about explosions and the English getting revenge on America's birthday, but let's move on. What did I know about condoms? I'd never seen one before that 4th of July afternoon. I'd previously been on the pill but was transitioning to a new doctor in anticipation of moving. The Englishman later confessed that the condom had been in his wallet for several *years*. Nine months and some change later, I was looking at the surprisingly self-aware mug of my Baby Boy.

When Baby Boy was one-year old, I found myself in Yorkshire, England. I was in the private dining room of an upscale country pub called the Saracen's Head. Baby Boy was tucked up in the nursery at his uncle's house while the grown-ups went out.

As I mentioned, I am always excited about meals, especially ones with white tablecloths. But at that time, I was unprepared for dinner with an endless budget and a rapid-fire delivery of adult beverages. When I was growing up in Southern California, I did not know anybody who drank alcohol. My father occasionally poured a scotch from an obscure bottle kept at the back of a cabinet, but I was more interested in bowls of ice cream drizzled with ribbons of chocolate syrup, my ten-year-old drug of choice.

The evening at the Saracen's Head did not start well. The other members of my party discussed how "Americans are so *direct*," like I was not sitting *right there*, so I was a bit jealous of Baby Boy relaxing in his crib at home. Next, when I took a stab at the pan-seared game bird appetizer—the slippery sucker turned out to be peacock breast—it skipped off my plate. In a last-ditch effort to avoid its fate, it skidded a foot across the table. *Oops.* I looked up shamefaced, but no one was paying much attention to the *direct American* by that point. Or they chose to ignore it with world-class English politeness. My inability to cut a game bird was one more bit of evidence that Americans are some species of barbarian. The interesting thing is that I have over 70% British ancestry—I had more British genes than some of the people at that table. But it turned out those things were the least of my worries.

I was seated between my brother-in-law and a family friend. The Englishman was at the opposite end of the table, sandwiched between the other ladies of the party. The family friend on my right was Big Bob, an outsized bon vivant well known in the county. Big Bob took pity on me. He leaned in, his beefy hands gripping fat-bottomed bottles of wine, heavy pint glasses of amber ale, and even delicate cut-crystal flutes of aperitifs that looked like miniatures in his big mitts. Throughout the night, he kept my glass full, or should I say, he kept many glasses full.

Big Bob, who had the only Ferrari I have ever ridden in, presented each new beverage with great conviction. Try this such-and-such vintage, young lady, and that so-and-so Bordeaux, my dear. This will pair well with that dish, my darling. As we've established: What did I know about drinking? I wasn't even legal drinking age in the U.S. yet.

Faced with glass after glass of wondrous liquids, I hadn't tiniest clue about the stamina required for this kind of gastronomic marathon. Were two drinks a lot? Were ten drinks a lot? This was years before I learned the trick of pouring drinks into a potted plant or down the toilet. To Big Bob, this was just another weeknight, and I was a trusting soul. I didn't really know what would happen if I took yet another drink from him, and then another. The sky might open, and all would be revealed, so I might as well pile on—down the hatch it all went.

Before that night, my only real experience with drinking was several months earlier on Baby Boy's first Christmas Eve. After dressing him in a tiny red-and-white Santa Claus outfit, complete with a pointy red hat, which was devastatingly cute, I discovered a bottle of Bailey's Irish Cream in the pantry where we were staying for the holidays. What I also discovered was that Bailey's tastes like a chocolate milk shake. Especially on ice. Almost an entire bottle of Bailey's later, after a bout of playing toss the tiny Santa Claus up in the air to make him giggle, I clapped him to my chest, and I sank into the couch. The ceiling spun a bit. But by some miracle, the aftermath of that night was not very bad. I could not have learned my lesson then.

Course one at the Saracen's Head started with a digestif of
sherry. Served in a miniature wine flute with a silver filigree
pattern, it was the color of a Victorian photograph. It was
sweet but dusty tasting. Big Bob poured me one and then
another. It coated the back of my throat, but it also made me
feel a bit jumpy like a speed freak at a metal concert. I craved
something salty to counter the sherry, which arrived in the
form of an extra treat from the chef, goat cheese puffs. They
were followed by an amuse bouche of cold cucumber soup in
tiny cups topped with a dollop of crème fraiche and a sprin-
kling of nutmeg. Crusty, fresh-baked country loafs were
brought out on wooden cutting boards, along with beautifully
carved butter roses to bust apart and slather on the thick bread
slices.

Course two (the one with the peacock) featured a rich,
dark-yellow Riesling. It was earthy like German summer soil
but refreshing. Glass one went down smoothly. Platters of
crudités appeared. I nibbled on carrots until the waiter placed
several large pots of foie gras pate on the table with a ka-thunk!
The foie gras had a rich, sharp bite. Big Bob was right—that
wine *did* pair well with that dish. He poured me a second glass
of Riesling. I shrugged. What the heck?

Between courses two and three, there was a hearty but
smooth local amber ale to "cleanse the palette." Big Bob regaled
me with stories of being chased around the county by the police
as he charged through the countryside in his red Ferrari. He
was clearly pleased with himself.

"That car deserves to be driven the right way," he said.
"Besides, I paid for the bloody thing, not the coppers. I pay
their salaries with *my* taxes."

"You know it," I said, nodding my head. I stabbed at the air
with my fork for emphasis.

At this point, my jealousy of Baby Boy getting to stay snuggled up at home had faded. I was in a gastronomic zone, excited to see what came next.

It was sheer heaven—a bacon-wrapped filet mignon medallion that was so tender that it practically melted into a puddle at the touch of my fork. It was like a stripper whose clothes fell off at the slightest glance. The filet was paired with a rich Bordeaux that had just enough acid to cut through the fattiness of the beef and bacon. That was glass number seven, by the way. Here's a fun fact for you: At the time, I weighed 98 pounds.

Here I was at one end of the table with Big Bob, while the Englishman remained at the other end entertaining the ladies with his stock anecdotes. They giggled; he also looked pleased with himself.

The first year of my relationship with the Englishman was fun. Then six months into the marriage came all the headaches —his, not mine. And there was the yelling, and the throwing of dinner plates when I was a minute late setting them on the table. There were the fists that used my arms as a punching bag. I wore long sleeves in summer to cover the orange-sized bruises. I wore long pants all the time to hide the welts from brutal kicking sessions inflicted with hard-bottomed leather shoes. I ignored the neighbors' looks when he locked me out of the house and threw my clothes out the back door. But I couldn't easily walk away. By then my parents were divorced. There was no place to go back to. And, by then I was pregnant.

I was distracted from this reverie by the next course, which was salad. Did you know that in France, they eat salad *after* the main course? *Huh. But this was England.* By then, I really didn't give a fuck. I could have been served rhinoceros steak and said, "Ooo, bring it on."

I was on drink eight or nine. The Englishman looked like a tiny bug at the other end of the long table. It was like peering at him through the wrong end of a telescope—or, rather, a kaleido-scope—broken, disjointed, sharp.

In Europe, meals always end with the cheese course. To this day, it is my favorite part. As I was reveling in the variety of Wensleydales, Barkham Blues, and Cheshire cheddars, the waiter walked up to me holding a silver tray. Apparently, Big Bob finally realized that I was out of my depth and ordered a pre-emptive remedy.

"Hair of the dog," the waiter said to me. I looked up at him, puzzled.

"I promise you, all will be well," the waiter coaxed, smiling confidently. He held the tiny glass towards me.

"Uh, no thanks," I said. "I've probably had enough." The English usually appreciate understatement, but the waiter was not convinced.

"This will prevent an 'angover in the moooor-nin," he crooned. "Ask Bob here." He nodded at Big Bob. "I promise you, lass," the waiter continued, holding the glass nearer my face.

"Go on," said Big Bob, "Get it down ya, lass."

The glass winked at me like a saucy lady of the night, and the dark-orange liquid appeared to shimmy in my direction. By the time the cheese course went down, I had sucked up not only nine *glasses* of alcohol of varying sizes, but also eight or nine *types* of alcohol. So, you can't blame me for being skeptical that this aperitif would cure a hangover before I even had one. It just didn't add up. It was a wonder that I could even see the waiter standing over me. The waiter, Big Bob cheering him along, was completely and truly convinced, after all I had to drink that night that this little magical glass of liquid would make it all okay in the morning. It was the key to making all future trouble vanish like so much mist in the night.

"Go on, then," the waiter smiled. He was cute. He meant

well. I took it, and I swallowed it down in one go. Who knew? Ten just *might be* the magic number.

Later at my brother-in-law's house, after a ride in the back of somebody's car alone —a taxi driver's, perhaps? —I rushed inside, stumbling upstairs to the nursery. "Baby? Where are you my Baby Boy?" I whispered in a sing song: "Baby. Baby. My baby boy. Baby, baby, baby boy. Boy baby. Ah, there he was —Baby Boy."

He was breathing softly as he slept in the crib of his aunt and uncle's tiny nursery. Their own sons had just been moved to their big-boy rooms. I gazed at this mound of onesie-clad love, his chest rising and falling. I wanted to nibble on his juicy limbs like a turkey leg. He stirred, perhaps smelling my scent. My milk surged at his gurgle. I picked him up. It was an entirely natural act. And it seemed entirely reasonable that I should lie down with him—right *there*—on the ugly wall-to-wall carpet of the nursery floor. As far as I was concerned, there was no place else in the entire world. Baby Boy and I were there, together, one. Baby Boy fed contentedly, while the room spun slowly around us.

Here is my final confession: There was no keeping it all down. By then, it was a surging speed train heading up from my stomach. Nothing could stop it—certainly not a hair of the dog sincerely offered by a cute waiter, certainly not just because that scale of drinking seemed so normal to everybody else. But I could not get up. I could not make it down the hall to the toilet. I didn't even think about trying. I just leaned to my right and let it fly away from Baby Boy. In the moment, it seemed like the right thing to do, like it had felt right to marry the Englishman two years earlier.

I held Baby Boy close, snuggled in my arms. I rolled over and went to sleep, my vomit spreading around us like a stain at a crime scene.

In the morning, I'd discovered that the Englishman never came home that night. He had gone off with the lady seated on his right. Due to my eruption in the nursery, my brother-in-law had to rip out and replace that ugly nursery carpet. I'd done them a favor, trust me. The Englishman had done me a favor, too. I could be free of him, and I could look forward to relishing other meals without him leering at me from across the wide expanse of a dining table.

PATIO

AMARA PHOENIX

I twiddle my keys in my right hand as I sit in the brown folding chair on my back patio. It's not so much a patio as a slab of concrete crudely covered with a metal roof that is propped up by flimsy metal rods secured to my neighbor's wire fence. The shoddy craftsmanship was courtesy of the previous homeowners and is now hidden by the wooden privacy fence my husband and I had installed three years ago. Now, you can only see the poor construction of my covered patio from the front yard. I try not to look at it. Surely, it's an eyesore, but nobody has ever complained.

I sit and stare at the rusty grey clock mounted to the brick on the side of my house just to the right of the sliding glass door that's currently boarded up against a hurricane that shifted at the last second. Tropical Storm Irma left our house completely unscathed and the $2000 we spent on hurricane preparation and evacuation was all for nothing.

The clock's hands are stuck at 3:10 because its batteries haven't been replaced since we bought it two summers ago.

We first saw that clock at World Market and my husband just *had* to have it.

"I like the look of that clock," he said.

"We don't need a clock. We have clocks on our phones," I said.

"I just think it'll look nice on the patio."

He picked up the clock, placing it in the shopping cart next to the packs of seasonally appropriate summer lagers and shandies I planned to partake in once we got home. I bought a pack of twinkling lights to go with the clock to make my tin-roof-covered concrete slab feel like a backyard oasis.

When we got home with our new clock and assorted beers, we let our five dogs out to run around in the backyard. We always followed our furry little stampede out of the house to watch them from our patio because our mutt Lucky figured out various ways to escape the yard. She could climb the old wire fence—the reason we got the new fence in the first place—and escape into the ditch behind our house. Now, she got out by crawling under the shed.

We'd supervise as the dogs frolicked. We'd smoke. I'd drink. I'd smoke some more. Time would tick by, hour by hour, and then became a blur. We knew to let the dogs in when the French Bulldog and pug's snorting became louder and more labored.

"Time for some water, puppies!" I'd shout as I let them in the house to get out of the South Georgia heat. If it was raining, odds are Karen, my German Shepherd, would come barreling around the corner, covered head-to-toe in mud.

"Only you, Kare Bear," I'd say while snapping photos, one of which I still share on Facebook every year on the anniversary of her death.

One or both of us would stay outside to finish whichever cigarette we were on. I'd stay outside and drink. I'd play on my phone. I might drunkenly text my friends. I might call Mom or my uncle to catch up and have someone to talk to. At least half the time, I'd go to call my dad only to remember that I couldn't because he was dead. For a moment, I'd feel like I lost him all over again. I might bring the tablet outside and play Sudoku until it became too hard. I'd leave more and more frequently to pee. My husband would come out periodically to smoke a cigarette or to let the dogs out again. As the summer evenings wore on, I'd start to notice how cute my dogs were.

"You're the cutest little pug in the world. Don't you think Mei is the cutest pug in the world?" I'd slur while snapping photos of her with my cell phone.

"She sure is, Sweetie," he'd say while shaking his head.

Periodically, I'd look up at the clock, closing one eye at a time to bring its hands into focus. I'd stay outside until it got dark, marveling over the cuteness of my dogs and creating a momentary ruckus as I discarded empty beer bottles into the recycling bin next to my chair.

Nowadays, I just come out here briefly to supervise the dogs, then go back inside straight away. It's been over a year since I smoked and drank on this patio. To be exact, it has been one year, two months, and 22 days. 64 weeks. 448 days. I know that because today is September 15, 2017, and I took my last drink on June 24, 2016.

Nothing crazy happened to trigger my quest for sobriety. There was no rock bottom. I woke up one day and realized that I drank an entire bottle of Grey Goose in two days, and it scared me. So, I just stopped. I quit smoking and drinking altogether. Cold turkey. Just like that. I told myself and everyone else that I did it because it was easier to stick with my fitness routine. Then I stuck with it because everything was easier without it.

Today, I lie back on the folding chair and stare at the tin

roof that never got decorated with that box of twinkly lights. The smell from the trash cans parked next to the chairs makes its way over to me, since trash collection got put on hold during the would-be hurricane. Every time I look at the cans, I remember that first July after we'd moved into this house, the one where I found my husband hunched over the cans, dressed in his Army uniform, and hyperventilating as the sound of fireworks boomed nearby.

"They're only fireworks. They're only fireworks. Sweetie, it's only fireworks." I repeated to him as many times as it took for him to believe it.

Now, I sit alone on this patio and the clock still reads 3:10 as I get up and walk through the yard to wrangle the dogs inside. There is a dirt path leading out to the yard from where my new shepherd Hank's paws have destroyed the grass as he leads the happy pack of dogs outside for potty breaks. The lawn is barely half-mowed in an indistinct zigzag pattern from where I started the job earlier this afternoon but stopped mid-mow when I saw a snake slither along the fence line.

"Nope!" I shouted indignantly as I threw my hands up in the air and left the lawnmower sitting in the middle of the yard.

I decided to forego the afternoon yardwork and began taking the hurricane boards off the windows instead. I started with the front of the house, removing the boards from the front door, the master bathroom window, and my bedroom window. When I got to the third window, I needed the ladder, which I'm normally discouraged from using due to my impossible clumsiness. I propped the ladder in front of the hedges instead of behind out of fear that more snakes were lurking in the bushes. With one foot on the ladder and the other on the brick ledge outside a window, I shakily removed the screws from the board using my husband's power drill. It wasn't an ideal position, but it was getting the job done until halfway through the fourth screw when I lost my balance and landed crotch-first in the hedges.

"God damnit," I shouted, angrily climbing out of the bushes as my neighbors looked on. When I finally emerged, I felt a tickle on my shin. I looked down to see a fat greenish yellow caterpillar crawling on my leg.

"Mother fucker," I screamed as I picked up a set of plyers— I don't recall why I had them or what I was using them for—off the pavement and started whacking indiscriminately at my own shin.

"Get off me. Get off me," I pleaded, swinging away, and drawing blood while my neighbors watched in amusement. The caterpillar finally fell off my leg on its own and crawled away unscathed as I went inside, shaking and out of breath. I needed to clean the self-inflicted gash on my leg. I left the back of the house boarded up.

Now, it's evening and my wounded shin is bandaged as I lead the dogs back inside, through the patio, past the clock that still read 3:10, and into the house through the garage side entrance.

"Good babies," I say, looking around my dark, quiet living room with its wall of windows entirely covered by plywood. I sit on the brown reclining sofa, still twiddling my keys. This is where I sat earlier this afternoon, before the lawn mower, before the caterpillar, right after my husband left. I held my head in my hands, sobbing as the front door closed and I heard the deadbolt lock behind him.

The evening before, we'd returned from my sister's house in Missouri. A few hours into our drive to Missouri, Irma had shifted and would not hit Savannah. We continued to Missouri anyway. I used his phone to input our destination into the GPS. I noticed he'd installed a sketchy messaging app on his phone.

"Why do you have Kik on your phone?"

"Oh uh, Jay must've put that on there."

The only thing more infuriating than his lies was how little effort he'd put into crafting anything even remotely believable. I opened the app to find a conversation between him and another woman, dated from a few months before when I was out of town.

"I'm attached so I have to be discreet as well," his message read.

"Do you like car play?" one of her messages replied.

It was an entire conversation between him and a stranger, making arrangements to meet and screw.

"No, love." I remarked pointedly. "This is you making plans to fuck someone while I was at school."

"No—" he stammered as he snatched the phone from me.

"You're a fucking scumbag," I said, shaking with tears in my eyes. He pulled into the nearest gas station.

"I want you out of my fucking house," I started. "I want you gone. I don't deserve this."

"I didn't actually meet her," he said.

"You're a fucking scumbag."

"If you actually look, it was probably a bot," he said.

"Are you fucking kidding me?"

"I wasn't going to do anything. I was just having the conversation."

"Fucking pig—"

"I was just getting off to the conversation," he said.

"So, either you cheated on me or you just got off to the idea of cheating on me. Which one is supposed to make me feel better?"

"I'm—I'm sorry."

"You're not, but you're about to be. Fucking scumbag."

"I'm going home."

"No, you're not."

"I'm not driving to Missouri with you like this."

"Fuck you. I'm not driving to Missouri all by myself with all the dogs and the cat."

"I'm not going to your sister's house like this."

"I won't tell her. But you're driving me. It's the fucking least you could do. When we get back, I want you out of my fucking house."

Our 13-hour drive turned into almost 20 with all the evacuation traffic. For 20 hours, we drove to Middle-of-Nowhere, Missouri: 5 dogs, 1 cat, 1 duffle bag, 1 frightened husband, and a seething wife all crammed into a Nissan Xterra. I blasted my personally curated music playlist crammed with such hits as Carrie Underwood's "Before He Cheats," Rhianna's "Take a Bow," and my personal favorite, Beyonce's "Irreplaceable."

This wasn't the first time something like this had happened. Every so often, there'd be something like this, and he'd give some half-assed explanation that was just so out there that it just might be true. *I was just searching for happy endings and nearby escorts. I only lied about the lighter in my car belonging to her because I knew you'd get mad. I only had a profile on that site so I could see the photos.*

Always a reasonable explanation. It just *looked* bad. He never actually *did* anything. Every time, I'd lose my shit and retreat to the patio, seething, chain smoking, and pounding Michelob Ultras or Coors Lights until it stung just a little less. Days of silent treatment and a verbal jab here and there would follow. I'd sleep on the futon in the guest bedroom because never in the almost ten years we'd been together had he ever been gentleman enough to surrender our bed to me, the wounded party.

It would end with me in a drunken stupor, sobbing and giving the same speech time and time again: "This looks really fucking bad. You do realize that if I choose to believe you, I will have to suspend all sense of disbelief and common sense as an intelligent human being, right?"

He would slowly nod at me like a scared puppy and promise not to do this ever again, though he inevitably would. In a few months' time, some app, some conversation, some shady search history would reveal itself, and we'd be right back where we started. Each time, I'd get even more enraged, and slowly, the rage would be directed more at myself and my own questionable judgment when it came to him.

A therapist will eventually tell us that all these incidents have nothing to do with me and everything to do with him and his own shit, and I won't care because while that may be true, it's always me who ends up getting hurt by it.

This time, I didn't waver. I held steadfast. We stayed with my sister for four days, and on the second day, after repeatedly being chastised by my sister and her husband for being short and irritable toward my husband, I told her what was going on. Since she's a more reasonable person than I, she comforted me, told me she supported me, and remained cordial toward my husband for the rest of our time.

When we returned home last night, he retreated to the futon in the guest bedroom and assured me he'd be gone in the morning. We could have just left it at that, but I didn't.

"Good. You're a fucking scumbag. Now you can screw around all you want."

"For fuck's sake, I told you I didn't do anything."

"Oh, I'm sure."

"I didn't fucking do anything," he screamed as he punched the end table. The thud made me jump, and I retreated to my bed.

The next morning—*this* morning—he packed his things and

loaded them into his car. He crouched down in the foyer and said goodbye to the dogs.

"Do you need anything before I head to Gramma's?" he said without looking up.

"No. I'm gonna mow the lawn because you're not gonna fucking do it."

"Okay. I'll come take the boards down this week if you want."

"Oh, I'm sure you will."

He said goodbye to the dogs once more and left. I cried into my hands, wondering how I ended up back here, though knowing full-well that it was always the things he did right that left me always forgiving all his wrongs. After all, he was the guy who stood with me on that patio almost five years before, trying to calm me down after I'd just found out that my father died.

"He's dead. Oh my god, he's dead. He died. He just died," I'd said frantically.

"What do you need?"

"I don't know. I don't know. I need to call my mom. And my sister. I need to call my mom and my sister."

"Take a breath, Sweetie."

"I can do it. I can do it. I can do it."

"Take a breath."

"Emergency leave. You can work on that. Go work on emergency leave so we can go. We have to go."

"I'm so sorry, Amara," he said as he went to hold me.

"Don't touch me," I screamed as I dialed my mother's number.

When he wasn't messaging random whores or Googling the closest rub-n-tug while I was out of town, he was texting me in the evenings on his way home from work and asking if I needed anything. He was fulfilling my request for "A six-pack of Michelob Ultra and some cigs," as I sat on the patio, three months after my father died, listening to nearly fifty old voicemails that I'd managed to recover from an old phone line we had in Germany while my husband was stationed there. He was the same guy who sat next to me, lighting my cigarette, opening my beer, and rubbing my back while my father's voice came over the phone: "I love you, Kid. Remember that. Always remember that I love you."

It's dark now. I take the dogs back outside and sit back down on the brown folding chair. I twiddle my keys as the porch light makes my keys glisten. Between my fingers, I pinch the keychain with the date 6-24-2016 engraved into it. Attached to it is a small circular charm with "1 year" etched on it. My mother and sister sent it to me after I'd made it a year sober.

"See, you can't start drinking again or else we'll have to get you a different keychain," my sister joked. They also sent me a custom-made leather-bound notebook with my initials, and I AM AN EXTRAORDINARY MACHINE printed on the cover. I know it was my sister's idea. She was supportive when I finally told her that I thought I might have a drinking problem.

"Wow. I had no idea."

"I don't think anyone did."

"I'm sorry."

"Me too. But I'm okay now."

My mother wasn't nearly as understanding.

"I didn't realize you had a drinking problem," she scoffed, sounding exasperated. Still, on June 24, 2017, I received these gifts from the both of them to commemorate my sober year. And I treasured them.

Now, I stare at my little rectangular keychain and think about the last week of my life. How, once again, my husband continues to engage in the same bullshit he always has and wondering how I can be so stupid as to imagine him doing anything different. I think about my muddy puppy amusing me on this very patio, and how less than two years later, I'd be lying on the floor of the vet office with her, saying goodbye and singing to her as she was being put down because life is just really unfair like that. I remember my mother screaming "What are you talking about?" in this long, drawn-out guttural cry and my sister's quiet, heartbreaking sobs as I stood on this crudely covered concrete slab and told them that Dad had died.

I get up from my chair and get in my car. I drive up the street to the convenience store and emerge from the store's walk-in freezer with a 12-pack of Michelob Ultra. I rest it on the counter of the register.

"Could I also get a pack of Camel Crush, please?"

I check out and drive back to my house. I put my case of beer in the fridge and take out two bottles, and I bring them outside with my keys, my phone, a lighter I found in the junk drawer, and my pack of cigarettes as I lead my dogs outside.

The low groans of my dogs playing together in the yard harmonize with the sound of the bugs, frogs, crickets, and whatever other little critters make noise at night. I remove the clear plastic from the black box of cigarettes, open the lid and remove the metallic piece of paper draped over the filters. I slide a cigarette out and place it between my lips. I bite down on the end to break the mentholated ball in the filter. I like these cigarettes because it gives you the option of menthol, but I always bite the end so I'm not sure why I need to have the alternative. Maybe I just like knowing I could take a different path if I wanted to.

I light my cigarette and take a long drag. I don't cough or choke. It feels like a breath of fresh air. As I sit on my chair, leaning over the small table where my beers and my smokes and phone and keys and lighter sit, I can't help but remember being a preteen and seeing my father sitting over the small table in my grandmother's basement during one of our weekend visits.

He'd sit there, flicking his Newport cigarette into an ashtray, surrounded by empty beer cans, listening to the radio. My sister and I would be lying on the futon in the corner that was held up by cinderblocks, trying to sleep.

"Sucks being alone, Kid," he'd say before taking another gulp of his beer and staring down at the table.

"I know. I love you, Dad."

"Love you too, Kid."

I've often wondered about Dad's relapses, and what he thought about before taking that first sip of beer after going so long without. For most of my life, I was convinced that he either didn't think of us at all before he did it, or he did, and it just wasn't enough. For a long time, it made me angry. For a long time, I saw his drinking as something he did to hurt us, as something he chose over us.

Now, I don't wonder anymore. I twist the cap off my beer bottle. The familiar hiss puts me at ease. I look at my keychain sitting on the table. I think of my sister. I think of how much I'll let her down. The keychain will be a waste now. How selfish of me. Over a year. One year, two months, 22 days. 64 weeks. 448 days. In a minute, all of that will be gone and I'll be back to zero. The stench of beer starts to overpower the trash smell. I like it. I take another long drag of my cigarette. So smooth.

I picture my sister's face. I remember her crying the day I told her about Dad dying. It was the second worst moment of my life, right here on this patio. I wonder how much it would hurt her to see me now. Surely, the second I take a sip of this, I will feel like trash. I will feel guilty and like a failure. I think about the last few days, about the moment I saw that chat transcript on my husband's phone. How he conspired behind my back to fuck a stranger. How he probably did it or he just *really* likes the idea of doing it. My heart starts racing. I take a nice big gulp from my beer.

It's ice cold, but as soon as it washes over my palate and spills down my throat, I feel warm. I am at ease. My heart isn't racing; it's beating steadily now. I feel no guilt or sadness. I take another swig and my first beer is almost gone. I feel warmth. Sobriety does not go out with a bang, but a whimper; that's another thing I've always been wrong about. I'm not thinking about anyone else now. It's not about anyone else; it's about me and how it sucks feeling so alone. There's no malice in my heart, only the desire to get away from this shit show for a little while. If there is some sort of equation or recipe for relapse, other people don't seem to factor into it.

I don't feel like trash. I don't feel like a failure. The night goes on, only briefly interrupted by my bathroom breaks and the sound of me tossing beer bottles into the recycling bin. I lie back on the chair with my beer and cigarette in hand. I close one eye and the clock comes into focus. 3:10.

This feels like home.

INDISCRETION

STELLA ALMAZAN

I grew up boy crazy.

My ardor took root as puppy love for celebrity pin-ups with their feathered hair and dreamy eyes. I fantasized about the stars of *Tiger Beat* magazine loving me in return as I kissed my pillow and hummed their names. As I moved into my teen years, my pining veered towards real boys, the sort who populated my town and classrooms. In my pubescent mind, boys were a badge of worthiness. Gaining their favor would indicate that I was suitable, accepted, desired.

But in little, ole Ridgedale, Pennsylvania, I was not made of the stuff that fed junior-high, straight-male fantasy. What they wanted was in that iconic poster of Farah Fawcett, flashing her knockout smile, with her big blonde wisps, big ta-tas, and teeny tiny waist in her teeny tiny red bathing suit. She was the all-American ideal of the day. I was the antithesis.

I resembled my brown-skinned, high-achieving parents who immigrated from the other side of the world. As their only child, they pegged all their hopes and dreams on me. And of course, they wanted me to be just like them.

They didn't fit in, though. Dad was the geeky town neurologist. Mom was a cranky physical therapist. An ingrained Catholic, she hoped I'd marry into our gene pool. She found genetic sameness comforting, as it implied cultural and religious conformity. She spurned the American way of life and its hedonistic trinity of sex, drugs, and rock 'n' roll. But for me, American assimilation was a life goal.

I felt a certain hopelessness. I was obliging and studious. My mother imposed a prim style on me to prevent pride or pregnancy. I grudgingly accepted my fate to be a spinster.

Then I went to the ninth grade Winter Holiday Dance.

In the junior high gym, my arms clasped Craig Archer's neck, his locked around my midriff. The aroma of freshly strewn sawdust mingled with clouds of Love's Baby Soft. He and I swayed ever so slightly to a Journey ballad in the dim light. In our minds, the other kids had faded away. Our fronts touched. His heart thumped against me. For the first time, I felt the solid expanse of male attraction at my waist.

Craig was my classmate in the gifted program. This cohort consisted of two girls and five boys. He was the most handsome of the group. He had thick brown hair, deep green eyes above his regal nose, and a stocky frame. He had a minor heart condition, which kept him from being a jock. So instead, he played saxophone in the band, aced history, and geography, and led the debate club.

Like me, he had a smarty-pants vibe that put off the cool kids. After morning bus drop, the Barbies and Kens stationed themselves at the far end of the gym for their fashion show and glib banter. At the near end, I found ease among the girls with glasses, and the other daughters of immigrants, who also felt the pressure for academic achievement. On the distant bleachers, Craig and a cadre of unobtrusive boys waited for the first bell in their own comfort zone. Winsome Craig, though, could have worked his way into being a cool kid if he had wanted.

Craig and I had engaged in weeks of gawky junior high flirting. In those days, that meant a lot of calling each other on the phone. At this dance, I couldn't believe our arms were at last around each other, and I was brushing my cheek to his peach fuzz. A moment later, our lips touched, soft and tentative, then pressing and dire. A swelling euphoria took over, lifting and spinning me. My first kiss was as thrilling as the ones I had seen on TV.

That kiss initiated Craig and me "going steady." I had my very first boyfriend. In junior high, dating consisted of sitting together on the bus and at the lunch table. We spent so much time together on the phone, our parents got mad at the tied-up household lines. Having a boyfriend also meant French kissing at dances while Craig held his enthusiasm against me, stretching the confines of his denim. My overprotective parents were not keen on me having a boyfriend, so I had to meet him there. I never let on what I was doing at these dances. I didn't want them to take away one of the most exciting things that had ever happened to me.

Our peers thought we were a good match. Ninth grade was the "senior year" of junior high when elections for "most popular," "best-looking," "most athletic," etc. took place. Male and female were selected for each category. Craig and I were voted "Most Likely To Succeed." We posed arm and arm for a yearbook photo. I worried what would happen if my parents ever saw it. But they never did.

Craig looked amazing in the picture. His hair was neatly combed. He wore his signature style— blue jeans and a V-neck sweater with a collared white button-down shirt underneath. The black and white snapshot did not flatter me. I had a weird hyperpigmentation and radiated awkwardness in my plaid blazer, half-permed hair, and hormone-fed lip fuzz. For Craig to like me was unfathomable, and yet exhilarating.

We were not quite 15. I was young, naive, and head-over-heels in first love. As far as I was concerned, I was going to marry Craig. He wanted something more, too, though.

One snow-day afternoon when my parents weren't home, I invited Craig to come over. He endured the elements and the walk to my house, down his hill and up mine. I was a bundle of anticipation wrapped in disobedient nervousness, but his kisses melted my uneasiness. We sat on the edge of my bed, tongues intertwined. He started taking off my blouse. Next thing I knew, he had my bra off, too, and his hand was on my naked, little boob.

It all happened so fast, my feelings were a jumble. I didn't want to stop him. I liked him. But I wasn't expecting this, and I wasn't sure I wanted it. Because what would come next? I knew I didn't want that. Why was he doing this? It had been fine the way it was.

"Craig?!" Frightened and baffled, I glared at him. His eyes bored into me with determination. Retreating into my good-girl cocoon, I started to cry. At that point, he ceased and desisted, and left.

A few days later, he broke up with me at school. I tried to put on my brave face, but as a young teen going through the intensity of facing her first time, that was futile. By English class, I broke down. Somehow, the teacher instinctively knew why I was sobbing. She came down the row and put her arm around me.

My first break up. Craig and I were together for three months, one week, five days, and 13 hours—the type of thing one keeps track of in junior high. My first love's ignominious end filled me with resolve never to get dumped again. I decided any future break ups would be my own doing.

After junior high, most of my classmates went to Ridgedale High. My mother deemed it "the big, bad public high school." She insisted that I go to Catholic school. In her world view, it would keep me chaste. She worried about "those heathen Protestant boys" preying on my virginity. Little did she know how horny Catholic boys are. Not that they ever hit on me, but I observed their ribald high jinks with all the pretty girls. Also, my mother did not understand the academics at the behemoth public high school were ten times better. A triple-A public high school could offer a lot more than a single-A private high school. But there was no arguing with my headstrong mother. So off to St. Agnes High School I went for a private, religious education.

During those years, the theater captivated me. I was drawn to the euphoria of being on stage. I studied the TV show "Fame!" as if it were a documentary guiding me to my professional future. Leg warmers, leotards, off-the-shoulder dance tees defined my style.

My tiny high school was not big enough to put on theater productions, but Ridgedale High had a booming program. I attended one of the plays there to see some actor friends from junior high. One unfamiliar actor mesmerized me: Ernie Pinsa.

His name sounded familiar. It dawned on me he had been my neighbor when I was a toddler. He lived in the house behind us in Brighton on the outskirts of Ridgedale. My family had a starter home there. My parents eventually built a house, and we moved to South Meadows when I was four. I hadn't seen Ernie since. The grown Ernie had a handsome, striking stage presence. He was a grade ahead of me. Already, these factors added up to irresistible appeal. The cast formed a receiving line in the lobby after the show. I approached cautiously.

"You probably don't remember me. I think I lived next door to you when we were little."

I could see the wheels turning in his mind. His enchanting smile creased his thick stage make-up. I suddenly felt myself floating. "You were great up there, by the way." I gestured back toward the theater.

Our friends watched us talking, nudging, and winking. That night sparked my high school, wildfire of a romance with Ernie. We did the standard teen dating scene: movies, pizza, dances. My parents watched with great consternation.

His parents had divorced and moved from Brighton. He now lived in Bilboa with his mother. That was the "wrong side of the tracks." Ernie had a bad boy reputation in Ridgedale circles. I never understood what the tracks were, or what that meant, or why he was considered "bad," but it heightened his mystique. Everything my mother was trying to avoid was coming to fruition. This made being with Ernie all the more tantalizing.

He was my dapper prom date. I attended two proms: his and mine. Then he caused a stir at my Catholic high school's Halloween dance. I dressed up as a princess, and he came in full Viking regalia, complete with a bare chest under a fur vest, horned helmet, and a full-sized spear. Alarmed, the strict, hulking chaperone clocked the weapon and a semi-nude male, and intercepted him like a bouncer. When the chaperone realized that the Norseman raider was with me, he reluctantly relented but kept a close eye on Ernie the whole night.

I'm with such a BADASS! My sheltered, dweeby teen ego swelled.

While having a notorious boyfriend was an adventure, the quiet moments with Ernie were my anchor. He paid attention to me and listened when I was sure no one understood my adolescent angst. He called me his precious angel, which made me feel, indeed, precious—but on my terms, not my parents'. When I was with him, I felt so special and close to him, I thought we'd be together forever.

As we continued to date, our group of common friends, thespian nerds, threw parties. My parents were comfortable with that. "How much trouble could there be at a party of nerds?" My parents didn't know these parties were teen orgies. We'd all pile into a room and neck and grope with our respective partners until curfew.

Another aspect made high school dating different—Ernie had a car. The parties became less frequent, but our love and hormones still churned. He found a spot in the East Side woods. Our dates became extended parking sessions. He respected my intent to not lose my virginity until marriage. So, we busied ourselves with everything except actual intercourse. Endless foreplay was strangely and madly more gratifying than going all the way would have been.

We continued to date through my senior year of high school even after Ernie had started at the university one town over. Then something shifted. Ernie got involved in a fundamentalist Christian church. I'm not sure why. Maybe it was in reaction to his tumultuous family situation or his poor adjustment to college. Perhaps he perceived his life as empty and meaningless, or his future hopeless and without direction as an actor wannabe. It seemed like he was searching for an attainable accomplishment.

Little by little, his behavior changed. What had been sweet and supportive conversations turned judgmental and controlling. He was certain everything he was doing now was right. He refused to be challenged. He drove us to an open field and made a big demonstration out of chucking his bong, which I didn't know he had. He threw away all his Blue Oyster Cult albums. My distress mounted. The final straw was when he no longer wanted to mess around because to him it was sinful. His religious conversion now affected me in a concrete way.

The final, final straw was he demanded that I recite Bible verses with him and declare my commitment to Jesus Christ. I was content with the Catholic sacramental rubric and wanted nothing to do with his newfound version of morality. It gave me the heebie jeebies.

The summer before I started college, I stopped going out with him. On a manual typewriter I tapped out a long letter explaining why we shouldn't see each other anymore. In essence, we were just too different. I fulfilled my prophecy from the Book of Craig—this breakup was on me.

I told my parents it was over. My mother tried to maintain a neutral reaction, but I knew she was dancing with delight on the inside. My father had the good sense to know Ernie and I would not be together forever and was relieved we had finally broken up. He was concerned, though, that Ernie might turn violent. Elements of Ernie's personality pinged his radar, but Dad did not share this worry with me at the time.

Like Ernie, I matriculated to the same university one town over. At the insistence of my parents, I had to forego the performing arts. They perceived theatrical pursuits as folly, so I took on a "respectable" major: engineering. On the first day, each student selected a desk, the student's chosen perch for the semester. But the during the second week of my Introduction to Engineering class, someone was in "my" seat. I plunked myself into an empty chair next to a stout, pigeon-toed fellow with feathery blonde hair. Because of this, he thought I liked him.

"You want to work on the assignment together?" He blurted in my direction as I packed up my books and notepads after the lecture.

I looked over to see the humble glimmer in his blue eyes.

"Sure, that would be great."

"I'm Matthew Mahoney."

"Do you go by Matt, or Matthew?"

"Matthew." He spoke with the wistfulness of someone with a common name trying to make it seem less common.

"Ok, Matthew." Oblivious to his come on, I slung my book bag over my shoulder and started toward the door.

He scurried after me. "I have another class now. But how's 4:00? I live at the Belfries. I believe there's a computer room on the first floor."

"Um, yeah. I'm over at Mildner, but that should work. See you then."

At the appointed time, I met him at his dormitory's computer center. We did our homework together that afternoon, then all the time. We started hanging out between classes. Matthew became a heartening homing beacon, a comfortable pattern. In this brave new chapter in my life, I appreciated his steady presence. I liked being around him.

Now that I was on the same college campus where Ernie was a sophomore, he began stalking me around campus even though we had broken up months earlier. I'd see Ernie lurking down a hallway from my classroom, or outside the library, or on the other side of the street from the campus shuttle stop. He wanted me to be aware he was around and knew where I was. As if this would win me back.

I felt secure having my new pal, Matthew, with me as my muscle. I told him what Ernie was doing, and Matthew kept an eye out. One day, Ernie got bold enough to board the same shuttle bus with me and Matthew. He sat in the back. The hairs on my neck prickled. I wondered what he was up to. Once we disembarked at the residence halls, Ernie followed us down the sidewalk. With Matthew backing me up, I spun around, hands on hips, and confronted my menacing ex.

Ernie babbled incoherently, alluding to my breakup letter.

He sneered at what he saw as my brazen and depraved life. He even bungled my name.

My eyes narrowed. Perplexed and full of pity, I took stock of him.

"Ernie, stop following me."

I swiveled sharply for emphasis and didn't look back. I took Matthew's arm and strode off. I wondered if Ernie's bizarre behavior could have been the first manifestation of mental illness. But I'll never know. I never saw Ernie again.

While Matthew had dazzling blue eyes, he was more ordinary than eye-catching—a bit chubby, with odd, Rodney Dangerfield mannerisms. It didn't matter to me. He was kind, and that superseded any sort of physical magnetism.

Winter break interrupted our daily habits. While Matthew was home in Annapolis, I missed our routine, the idle conversations, the silly ways we'd pass the time. I realized liked him a lot. I hand-wrote a love letter to him on yellow lined paper and signed it with a lipstick kiss. Matthew was floored but emboldened by the green light. We officially became boyfriend and girlfriend. Whether it was a weekday or the weekend, we spent all our time together. Matthew and I became increasingly affectionate. Cuddling turned into kissing. Kissing turned into fondling. Fondling turned into petting. We rounded the bases fast and furious but held up at third where my Catholic school mores stood defense.

While I struggled to contain my yearnings for Matthew, I went on retreat with a group of students from the university parish. Episcopalian Matthew did not come along.

During reflection time, I ambled away from the retreat house to a distant corner of the property. A buddy, one of the sophomore guys, joined me. He and I sat on a patch of grass and stared at the stars. Side by side, we spoke sort of to each other and sort of to the cool night air.

"What do you think about having sex before marriage?" I sighed as if I had let go of a heavy burden. "Do people really go to hell for that?"

To me, it seemed silly to get married just to have sex. That was more customary in our parents' day. I saw it as a sure set up for divorce.

"Well, I haven't exactly been an angel in that department."

I listened to his admission with some surprise. He came across as a choir boy, albeit a good-looking one.

"Hmmm." I nodded in acknowledgement. My mind wandered back up to the inky sky, absorbing his brotherly confession as my absolution.

A month later, there were no classes on Good Friday. On his dorm room bed, Matthew and I clumsily plunged into our mutual rite of passage. It didn't hurt. I didn't bleed. Much to my chagrin, Matthew had broken my hymen with his fingers a few weeks earlier. There had been so much build up to this moment. But even with a condom, the ultimate experience lasted only two seconds. Our love, though, grew long and strong.

We grew as people, too, often driving each other to bloom and prosper.

We both changed majors. I switched to physics, Matthew to political science. I became a campus ambassador for prospective students; he became an R.A. in the residence halls. I admired Matthew's interpersonal savvy. Even though he was a little dorky and an average student, he was an effortless leader and manager. He ran for student government. I gleefully helped as his campaign director. He won the colossal Belfries precinct by a landslide. I could tell that politics was his destiny. I envisioned us as a power couple. His success and ambition held me spellbound. As I lay in his sheets one afternoon, I thought, *I'm making love to the future President of the United States, and I'm going to be First Lady.*

After college graduation, we continued our love affair. He moved on to law school at Widener University south of Philadelphia. With top honors in physics, I went to medical school in Hershey. We spent weekends traveling between the two cities to see each other. I loved him enough to carry on our long-distance romance, enough to marry him. I figured if it was going to last forever, waiting a few years wouldn't matter. We viewed each other as key to our future aims and achievements. Saying goodbye on Sundays hurt every time as he looked at me with devotion. I shut my apartment door with a little swoon. *I love him so much.*

Matthew, the politician, inspired my political proclivities. In med school, I became happily embroiled in the Medical Students of America, a national medical advocacy organization. At the semi-annual national meetings, medical students representing schools across the country worked together to analyze resolutions, develop talking points, defend positions, schmooze, and influence. Some students had more influence than others.

"That Adam Lyons, mm, mm, mm." The beautiful Christine from Tennessee licked her lips. "He can sway me any time."

Adam Lyons attended the Uniformed Services University of the Health Sciences, the national military medical school in Bethesda. He was Navy like he was cast by Hollywood—tall and muscular, cropped light chestnut hair, clean shaven, sexy as hell, and even sexier when his stubble peeked through.

I overheard many attractive and accomplished female colleagues at the MSA meetings praise Adam, from the plucky Melinda from Wisconsin to the elegant Jamie from Indiana. He flirted with everyone but committed to no one. With my cropped dark hair and cafe au lait complexion, I put myself out of the competition. In my estimation, I didn't stand a chance with him. All the while, he mercilessly stirred my lust and occupied my thoughts. Besides, I had a boyfriend. So, I simply enjoyed being his friend, colleague, and meeting collaborator.

Many state delegations marked the end of the MSA meetings with "hospitality parties" in the various suites of the convention hotel. "Hospitality" was code for open bar. The students from Pennsylvania and Maryland ended up at the Texas celebration. There the white-hot presence of Adam Lyons ignited my cravings. He and I had a spirited tête-à-tête at a back table before my cohorts dragged me into the core of the soiree.

At 24, imbibing was still novel to me. I had been a goodie-two-shoes, even through college. After several glasses of hospitality, I was tipsy. Not fall-down, slurred, and sloppy, but cute, activated, giggly.

"Does anyone have a condom?" I tittered, like a bad girl wannabe. I flitted from friend to friend among my Pennsylvania cronies, my conference besties. They knew me well and found my inebriation amusing. I didn't really expect anyone to have one. I was shocked when a handsome medical student from Pittsburgh pressed into my palm a disc enclosed in a square of plastic.

"Have fun!" he whispered and winked. A couple of my schoolmates from Penn State watched and chuckled.

The party wound down. Adam and I locked eyes across the crowd of departing revelers. *Does he know how much I want him?* We left, too, and sneaked upstairs to his room. As the door clicked shut behind us, he put his arms around me and clamped his mouth to mine. I tiptoed to meet his lips, sweet with booze. With his body against me, he coaxed us toward the bed.

"Give me a second." I paused and slinked away into the bathroom. My head was still pleasantly swimming with hospitality. I looked at the gift in my hand. I looked at my reflection in the mirror. *Is this really happening?*

Not wanting to be presumptuous, I emerged tentatively from the bathroom in my lingerie. Adam had already slipped into bed and pitched a captivating tent. I sauntered over and handed him the condom. He grinned cheekily and raised an eyebrow. "I'm very proud of you." As doctors-to-be in the early 90s, safe sex wasn't only lip service. He swiftly donned the prophylactic and drew me on top of him.

My drunken and inconceivable one-night stand with Adam became a distant memory. To ease my guilt, I chalked it up to cocktails and opportunity. With this crude rationalization, any remorse I felt about the incident evaporated. I didn't mention my fling to Matthew. It had simply been a spontaneous, one-time, flaming-hot indiscretion.

With his oozing charisma, Adam brandished some power in convention circles. I did, too, with my hard work and connections. I got elected to national office on the MSA Board of Governors. When summer rolled around, I vacationed with Matthew's family at his father's beach house in Tallahassee. An MSA acquaintance paid me a social call while I was there. He was a med student from the Florida State University delegation.

In the living room, the three of us engaged in pleasantries. No ostensible political agenda emerged, but it didn't have to. At least, not yet. This was the business of politics. At a moment of levity, I glanced over at Matthew. Instead of a laugh, he sported a tight-lipped simper, the color of deep, green envy. He was jealous that I was the one being lobbied, not him.

As I discharged my duties of office, I figured out I enjoyed the campaigning more than the responsibilities. The messaging and the public speaking were more invigorating than the nitty gritty of making policy. Because of this insight, I went to campaign management school coordinated by a political action committee in Washington, D.C. In the one-week intensive, immersive course, participants ran a tabletop campaign simulation. I was hooked. I was sure I wanted to pursue political campaign management professionally someday. I shared my lessons with Matthew. I was stunned that he didn't seem to get it. The concepts were too obtuse for him. What was obvious to me he found stupefying.

My perceptions of him started to change then. My disdain increased as he internalized the content of his tort law classes. He derided the carelessness of doctors. It struck me as adversarial.

In the last semester of med school, I had the opportunity to do a rotation in rare diseases at the National Institutes of Health. On a student budget, hotels in the capitol corridor were out of reach, especially for a four-week stint. I called Adam, who lived in Bethesda.

"Hey, I need a place to stay." I hoped he'd offer me the couch, or even the living room floor for me and a sleeping bag.

"Well, you can stay here. It's a one-bedroom apartment, but you're welcome to share my bed."

WOW! An offer I couldn't refuse.

Sharing Adam's flat was like living in a romance novel. Seduction slithered at every turn, even when he didn't intend it. As I watched from the kitchen table, he pulled his uniform out of the dryer.

"As you know, I don't wear underwear with my dress whites."

Yes. I did know. No visible panty lines on his fine ass. That aspect of his anatomy, along with all the others, never escaped the notice of the young women of the MSA, including me, who was now his bedmate. *Eat your hearts out, ladies!*

As hormonal 20-somethings, I thought Adam and I might

have sex every night. Over the four weeks, it turned out to be only an occasional thing. Despite the mind-blowing shags, I knew I wasn't his girlfriend. I did not expect more than I was given. We were friends with benefits, which was a satisfying arrangement. In the throes of medical school, we faced similar pressures—our grades, the future, the elusive work-life balance. I made dinner and did chores around the apartment. He helped me figure out how to rank my residency choices. Symbiosis at its best. While I loved it, I knew it wouldn't last. I would have to go.

On the final night with Adam, he said, "Wanna go for a ride?"

His proposition intrigued me. I'd never ridden on a motor-cycle before. He wrapped his puffy down jacket around my small frame. He tugged at the front closure to snap it securely around me. Next, he retrieved a plain white helmet, carefully placed it on my head, and tightened the straps at my chin.

"To keep you warm and safe." Firm, yet affectionate.

I acknowledged his charming concern with a nod. My eyes met his, deep and reflective, bright, twinkling, crystal blue. My gentle footsteps echoed his sturdier stomps down the flight of metal stairs. I climbed on the back of his Harley. As we sped down MD-355, I felt the exhilarating roar between my legs. The plane of our heat sliced the winter wind. I clasped his leather-clad back against my chest.

We came back to the apartment and peeled off our cold layers. He laid me down on his warm bed and spread me out like a blanket. He tenderly lavished love upon my hungry lips. He slid himself inside me, and we melted together one last time. *What am I doing with this guy? So out of my league.*

And yet...I was doing this guy, so out of my league. My dalliance with Adam made me think, *If I can have a guy like Adam, I can have any man I want. Why am I settling?*

I had come a long way from my awkward child-of-immigrants days. I had academic and political success. Adam, the Ken doll of my psyche, was the final badge of worthiness. I felt suitable, accepted, and desired as a young woman.

Matthew never knew the full details of me sharing Adam's abode. He assumed I was sacked out on the sofa. What he didn't know wouldn't hurt him. But my experience with Adam forced me to question my relationship with Matthew. Adam was an affair, a symptom of dissatisfaction. Despite a true love, I had grown weary of Matthew, a frumpy B student. He had great ambitions but only a superficial understanding of what was important *to me*. I returned to Hershey to finish med school. Over the next several months, I mulled over my situation, and my feelings for Matthew disintegrated.

Much to my disappointment, Adam was not at the next MSA meeting, which would be my last. I drowned my sorrows by palling around with a schoolmate, Dom Pinsola. Along with a dozen other medical students from the Penn State College of Medicine, he and I represented our school and the Commonwealth. We admired each other as movers and shakers within the organization. Cooperation and victory fostered our friendship.

Dom and I shared some good-natured flirting during our MSA travels, but nothing ever came of it. Like a pleasant game, it felt good to exchange coy glimpses with the smart and poised Dom across the table or room. His striking, dark eyebrows drew me into his mellow, brown eyes. He was beguiling and handsome in a boy-next-door-who-went-to-med-school kind of way.

Our next conference was in Honolulu. At the end of business, the Pennsylvania delegation of mid-20-somethings indulged in customary celebration at the hospitality suites, and then at the local bars, clubs, and sights. But now in my late 20s, I had grown weary of the partying, even though it made me temporarily forget about real life and the turmoil I felt about Matthew. After carousing for a while with the group, Dom and I split off and found ourselves beachside next to our hotel.

Dom, a button-down-and-khakis-kind-of-guy, had his sleeves and pant legs rolled up. The gentle breeze mussed wisps of his short, straight blond hair. Walking barefoot on the beach together melted away the convention stress. The waves of the Pacific crashed gently. The palm trees overhead swayed in the starlight. It seemed perfectly natural for our lips to meet. Our kisses grew more passionate and insistent. He urgently pressed in with his tongue, met hungrily by mine. My bosom swelled against his virile body. His big hands firmly caressed my back and hips. His thickness at my waist prodded my need for him.

As far as we were concerned, we swirled in this trance alone. But we weren't alone. Though we were cloaked in the night, skyscraper hotels loomed above us. An occasional passerby strolled the beach. A random car pulled into the nearby parking lot. Although we wanted to continue this tryst elsewhere, we had a dilemma. On this expensive trip, we had packed as many people as we could into each hotel room, six girls in mine, six guys in his. We had nowhere to go.

After an eternity of kissing and burning desire, it became apparent nothing beyond second base was going to happen. If we were going to do this, we were going to do it right. Not a quickie on the sandy beach without a towel. Not a skinny dip with sea creatures only to wriggle our wet bodies back into our clothes.

So, we called it a night. We sat on a concrete barrier at the edge of the parking lot to put our shoes on. Beneath the light pole in the harsh glow, Dom gazed at me with gentleness, as if he were beholding a graceful swan.

"You are a beautiful woman."

His soft, appreciative whisper moved me with all the power of Cupid's arrow, like an I-love-you without the specific words. At that moment, I loved that beautiful, young man, too. Dom and I parted ways. Life and medicine carried us to different cities and careers. He faded into a tender memory.

Matthew's three years of law school and a year of clerkship came to an end. The rigors of four years of med school were over for me, too. The next step was residency, a time of tumult and cataclysm. For Matthew, it was time to join a firm, settle down, and start a family. I was far, far away from that.

When I arrived for a residency at the Greater Baltimore Medical Center, Matthew came to help me unpack. He thought we could finally cement our relationship since we lived closer together again. However, I had already been pulling away from him for months.

"Matthew, I- I can't. I don't think we should see each other anymore," I stammered, my voice cracking. He sat heavily down on one of the empty boxes.

"What?" he exhaled.

"I thought...I always thought we'd get married." His voice trailed off.

"Now's not the time!" I played up annoyance to make the split easier.

I knew he'd have no patience. He wanted to get on with his vision for his future. The pointlessness of continuing our relationship dragged on my soul as I stood on the cusp of becoming the adult me. Everything about my life and my identity was in flux. It was hardly the moment to take an enduring vow. But this unavoidable pain had deterred me from breaking up sooner.

With this brief exchange, eight years of dating came to an end. We had been so in love, but over the last six months, we simply drifted in different directions. We were on opposite sides of a widening chasm. Matthew flew off in his red sports car straight to a party in Delaware. Afterwards, I found out later, he sat alone in his car and wept, while I sat alone in my new apartment where I wept, too, with only moving boxes to keep me company.

After residency, I married a brilliant and muscle-bound orthopedic surgeon. We put down roots in Juniata County. I divided my time between private practice and teaching ophthalmology at the Penn State medical school. I also helped start an ophthalmology program at a newly established medical school in Tajikistan.

After several years of being settled down in my adult life, Dr. Jay Mulroney from the med school's Office of Student Affairs gave me a call. He was a fellow Penn State Med graduate. He reached out on behalf of a secret alumni group, the Keystone Club. The invitation-only society tapped Penn State Med alums who did noble, notable, or interesting things with their careers. Heads of departments, outstanding educators, and a doctor for the homeless graced its roster. Jay invited me to join the group for my unusual vocational pursuits. The group met quarterly for dinner and a lecture by one of its members. The meetings were steeped in tradition. They took place at the Union Guild, a private social club near the state capitol. The dignified old building featured splendid architecture outside and aging grandeur inside: lots of masculine wood paneling, ornate patterned carpet, imposing chandeliers. Every February, the Keystone Club gathered in black tie, formal attire. At this February meeting, I would be inducted into the club.

Medicine is a small world, and everyone had a hazy mental map of who's who and where. I was vaguely aware that Dom, now a gastroenterologist, had settled back in my area. The night of my induction, I strode into cocktail hour in a long, elegant, black evening gown. I had no notion that Dom was already a member. I held in a gasp as I spied my former paramour chatting with a few of the other doctors at the far side of the bar. His hair was shorter and now a grayish, dark blonde. He was decked out in a tuxedo. He had one hand in a pocket and a drink in the other, looking debonair and sublime. My carefully packed away memories of him tumbled out of my heart.

He didn't see me at first, but when he recognized me, his eyes grew as big as saucers. We hugged. He gave me a peck on the cheek. I was disappointed he wasn't more slyly affectionate. Did he not recall our night in Hawaii? Was it not a fond memory?

At dinner, I sat between Jay and Dom. When the time came for my rite of installation, Jay asked Dom to make my introduction. I was taken aback. I had assumed Jay would do the honors, since he had extended the invitation. Dom stood up in his quiet, confident manner. He extemporaneously imparted the highlights of my résumé. He smiled warmly and welcomed me into the fold. Courteous, assenting applause ensued.

This turn of events puzzled me. How did he know my accomplishments so well?

Dom winked. "Jay warned me you'd be coming. He knows we're old friends." I opened my mouth to press him on that, but he immediately launched into small talk: How are you? How's work? How's the family?

At a pause in the conversation, I eyed my cocktail glass. The servers had brought everyone the standard, traditional aperitif, a Manhattan: whiskey, vermouth, bitters. Dreadful stuff. Tasted like cough syrup, only worse. I had only sipped at mine so far, but now I took a hearty swig.

I turned to Dom with that familiar, coquettish glance from years gone by. "You know, someday, you and I should finish what we started."

"Yeah, we should." With one raised eyebrow, he matched my playful look.

The delicious moment I had been lusting for.

He *did* remember! I *wanted* him to *remember*. I wanted *us* to remember *together*. To feel that lovely tension once again, to acknowledge that beautiful night we shared with each other so many years before.

The memory cast a momentary spell, but I had no intention of getting into Dom's pants, and I did not believe he truly wanted into mine. Perhaps in a fantasy world, but not in the real one. I had already experienced the aftermath of indiscretion. Now more mature, I thought better of pursuing the physical act.

When I got home, my husband was getting ready for bed.

"How was the dinner?" He mumbled, toothbrush against his teeth. In the bathroom mirror, his hazel eyes twinkled, his rusty eyebrows shooting up at the reflection of me in my evening finery.

"Great! Saw some old friends." I shimmied out of my chic trappings and pulled on a nightshirt. "It was kind of fun to remember who I used to be."

"Do you wish you could go back?" He spit out his toothpaste with a smirk.

I thought about the "almost" between Dom and me. What if Dom and I had consummated our passion that night under the palm trees? Would my memory of that night be different? Probably. I now knew that the delicious recollection of unfinished business was the sweeter meat. The mere thought of Dom was a grander, more valuable treasure without the complicated outcomes.

"No." I answered my husband slowly. With a washcloth, I wiped the makeup from my pensive face. "It was all fine back then. But I like me better where I am now."

We crawled into bed. He caressed me through the thin fabric of my chemise as he huskily whispered in my ear. "I like you better where you are now, too." Feeling a reciprocal urge, I jostled my cheeks against his advances.

As we made love, flashes of my past flames flickered in my mind. The fun parts. The heady, lusty bits. Blissful spasms rippled deep inside me as I gripped my husband. He fell asleep quickly afterwards. I stared at the ceiling thinking about my romances, who I had once been, and the choices I made. I couldn't see any other way those scenarios could have played out. It occurred to me that I was happiest when what I wanted most was almost in my grasp but just out of reach. Sometimes, love is best unfinished.

THIS TIME FOR GOOD

JOSEPH BECK

I had just finished my second year as a high school English teacher, and I was exhausted. During the last week of school, my 15-month-old son, Ralphie, was teething and decided to keep my wife Renee and I up a few hours each night. So, in the morning I'd drag myself out of the house, teach all day at JFK High School, coach, attend night classes at Queens College for my master's degree, then go home to grade more papers before collapsing in bed. This had gone on for months.

On top of this, we were struggling to pay our bills. When Ralphie was born, Renee decided to stay home with him. To work didn't make sense; the cost of day care was nearly half her salary from her job as an editor of physics journals.

So, there we were, in debt, the junkyard crooking a finger at my 12-year-old Nissan, and tenure, a virtual ticket to lifelong job security, was still a year away and not guaranteed. I started to ask myself: *Why do I work so hard? Why do I push myself? When do I get time for me?* Some mornings I cried my way to school and longed for the carefree days when Renee and I dated.

I met her on her nineteenth birthday. I opened the door to my dorm room at Oneonta State University and there she was in faded jeans held together with patches. She had a mane of strawberry blond hair and the warmest brown eyes I had ever seen. I eventually asked her out, and we found we both loved Shakespeare, Chinese food, and Woody Allen movies. A year after graduation, we got married. I was very happy.

Now, 12 years later, everything had changed. When we weren't fighting about money and the stress of being parents, we ignored each other. After a while, I began to wonder if staying married was worth it.

School ended on a Friday in late June and whatever our differences, we both looked forward to a weekend picnic with friends. On Saturday morning, though, Renee didn't feel well and wasn't up for the picnic. Her legs felt like iron. Her skin was clammy, and she looked pale. I took her to a nearby clinic because our family doctor didn't have hours on Saturday. A doctor examined her and sent her home. She spent most of the day sleeping on a couch in the living room while I wrote lesson plans in the next room.

About four o'clock I heard Renee moan, then nothing. I rushed into the living room, just as she moaned again. Then, horribly, she began thrashing wildly, then stopped. I called 911 and waited for the ambulance. They came and carried her out and into the ambulance for the trip to the hospital. On the way, the paramedic repeated my wife's name "Renee, Renee!" as he worked over her. "Can you hear me?" Renee moaned and uttered unintelligibly. Then, he fired a string of questions at me: Prior seizures? Illegal drug use? Smoker?

"No." I said, overcome with fear, anger, and tears. "Can we just get to the hospital?"

"We're doing the best we can, sir. We'll be there in about six minutes."

Renee's parents arrived a few minutes later. My sister-in-law, who lived upstairs from us, had called them. A doctor told us that Renee was still unconscious, and her seizures were increasing in severity and duration.

The anti-seizure drugs dampened but would not quell the seizures. The three of us sat in the waiting room, numb. Finally, a doctor told us what they knew so far. Renee was having "intractable" seizures. Nothing, not even drugs, could stop this type of seizure for more than a short period and they were worsening. *What was happening? Was she going to die?*

She didn't. For the next five days, doctors ran every conceivable test on her. They all came back frustratingly normal. Still, seizures broke through every powerful drug. Something had to be done. The doctor told me she might be headed for a place from which few return: status epilepticus. This is when seizures come so frequently, they are, for all intents and purposes, constant.

On the morning of the sixth day, the doctor looked at me. There was nothing more they could do for Renee and the only chance they had for saving her life was getting her to Columbia Presbyterian Hospital in Manhattan, right away.

Dr. Stephan Mayer, head of the Neuro Intensive Care Unit (NICU) at Columbia Presbyterian Hospital, admitted Renee when she arrived. By this time, Renee's brain was practically on fire, convulsed in horrific, non-stop seizures. If he could not stop the firestorm, her brain would burn out—if it had not already.

Out of all the drugs they had tried, one possibility remained, risky enough that few neurologists tried it. It was the barbiturate pentobarbital. Dr. Mayer gave Renee a mega dose. The idea was to hammer her brain's neurons into silence and suppress its electrical activity into flat lining, the electrical equivalent of being brain dead. The idea was to smother the seizures, then slowly bring her back, but they might not be able to. She could die.

During all this, I traveled to Manhattan to read to her and hold her hand, even though she was in a coma. Later, I'd go home and straighten up the house, do some yard work, and make the kid's lives as normal as possible. I explained that mommy was tired and just needed a rest.

Later, friends asked, "How did you hold it together?"

Healthy brains have a remarkable capacity for detachment, but not all the time. In my mind, Renee was just away for a few days. I remember one incident in particular. I was watering the lawn, and I remember thinking it was really coming up nicely this year. I looked over on the deck and noticed a book she had been reading. It was open, turned over, and her favorite bookmark was just where she left it. My chest suddenly deflated, and it was hard to breath. I sat down and sobbed uncontrollably. *What am I going to do if my best friend dies?*

For the next few weeks, she remained in flat line, somewhere between life and death. They tried to bring her up three times. More seizures. They pushed her down again. A few weeks became many weeks. They told me I made 62 trips to Manhattan in 63 days. I just wanted to see Renee. I read her Shakespeare and Maya Angelou, her favorite poet, held her hand, and played her favorite music for her. I so desperately wanted her to wake up.

Then, one morning in late August I was getting ready to leave for the hospital. The phone rang. A crying nurse was on the other end. Renee was awake and asking for me. I don't remember the trip to the city that morning. I do remember approaching her bed. She was sleeping. When I touched her hand, her eyes slowly opened, and she lifted them to my face. Her tracheotomy helped her to breath but wouldn't allow her to talk, and neither could I. She managed a faint smile and as she did, the skin around her brown eyes relaxed and softened.

It was hard to believe but there she was. For the first time in a long time, it all came back to me. She was just this girl who never wore makeup or needed it, and her beauty drove me to distraction. Standing by her bed that morning, I started to love her again and to realize how desperately important she was to me. I felt powerful, vulnerable, and alive, all at the same time. Since then, Renee has made a nearly complete recovery. I know I have. At some point during this whole thing, I fell in love with Renee—again—and this time for good.

OVER, UNDER, ROUND AND ROUND

PHYLLIS PETERSON LEVINE

The casket is a strange size, too small for a person and too big for a child. A piece of cloth, a pale, cream-colored fabric, is draped over the casket. It flutters with the breeze as a single, moon-colored horse pulls the wagon holding the odd-sized casket. A crowd of hooded figures move to give the horse a clear path making its way to a robed priest standing beside a deep hole. On cue, the horse stops when it reaches the priest. There is a long silence. The camera pans out, rising above the scene, then focusing on the priest's moving mouth, but I can't hear what he's saying. And then a roar of laughter rises from the crowd standing around the small, open grave.

"What a lousy beginning to a movie," I say. "Why would people laugh at a funeral?"

"I thought it was pretty good," Dan says. "The laughing makes it intriguing. People don't normally laugh at funerals."

Why would Dan find that intriguing? Funerals aren't funny. Especially right now. Hospitals are full of dying people. There are so many they're putting them in refrigerator trucks. I can't stand to watch the news anymore. I think I'd go mad if it

173

weren't for these movie nights. So here we are again: me and Dan self-isolating on another Saturday night watching movies at my place. I touch my ring. Ray's been gone almost three years. Dan wasn't wearing his ring the night we met. His wife has been gone longer. I grab the remote and pause the movie with the dumb name, *The Casket*.

"What's in the casket, do you think? It's such a tiny thing," Dan says.

"You said you went to an actual funeral today? How many people were there?" I ask.

"Are those figures men or women? I can't tell," Dan says as he stares at the frozen TV screen.

"How many people were there?"

"Around the casket?"

"Not in the movie. At the funeral you went to today."

"Oh yeah. That. There were quite a few but everybody wore a mask, especially since that one guy died of COVID that she worked with."

I'm pretty sure the county health department said no more than ten should congregate. I want to tell Dan to go home. What is he thinking? Does he even care about me? I can see colorful, barbed virus spheres floating in the air. Strangely, they remind me of sperm. That would make me an egg. I'm a pretty good egg.

"Did you wear condoms? I mean masks?"

"Huh?"

"It's a joke."

"Condom, huh?" Dan smiles momentarily. "At first, and then we went outside, and they all came off."

I can see a bunch of men standing around outside a funeral home taking off condoms. Dan's got his eyes on the TV and doesn't see me smiling. And then he says, "What could be in that casket? And what were they all laughing at?"

It was going to be a dumb movie. I shouldn't say that. That's making a snap judgement. Not being open. Pigeonholing it as a commercial, slick movie. I need to give it a chance. Maybe explain to myself why I thought the movie was going to be dumb. And I shouldn't use the word dumb. Maybe a better word will come to me. But there was something about that first scene. It was the odd size of the casket. It did get me wondering what could be inside. And the laughing after the horse stopped and that guy talked. What a twist. That first scene wasn't just a hook, it was a big, ole fishing net. The kind that pollutes the oceans. That's what it was. It was gimmicky. The scene was big enough to drag everyone in. A summer blockbuster. And Dan likes it. But does he like me? I bet someone at the funeral had the virus.

"You want me to open the wine now?" Dan asks.

"No, that's okay. I'll get it."

It was nice that he brought wine, but I had to wash the bottle to get all the COVID spheres off. I don't want him touching my glass.

"You want some popcorn?"

"Sounds good."

I resent waiting on him. We met about a year ago, and it feels like we're in a 1955 marriage.

Dan comes into the kitchen while I make the popcorn.

"So, how was the funeral? Did you feel safe, you know, with the COVID and all?"

"Yeah, pretty much until we went across the street to the restaurant."

Damn it. I know they didn't wear masks in the restaurant. I divide up the popcorn, salt mine, and give Dan the shaker. We sit back down. Well, that does it. I'll probably get the COVID while Dan breathes, and we watch this damn movie. I wish we were watching a better movie.

"Can I hit continue?"

"Yeah, here's your wine."

Now *Ghostbusters* was a great movie. Right from the beginning scene. It starts out in a library. I love libraries. I worked in a library. Coincidentally, I shelved books like the lady in the first scene in *Ghostbusters*. I must admit that it was kind of spooky when I went down in the basement of the library to shelve. That's where they kept the old reference books and newspapers that didn't circulate.

"Oh look, they found it in a lake," Dan says, his eyes on the screen.

"What is it?"

"I don't know. Is it a kid? It was so quick when they pulled it out. I couldn't make out what it was."

My eyes feel itchy. I hope this isn't the beginning of coronavirus symptoms.

"Uh huh." I stare at the screen.

"What did he say?" I ask.

"Something about a dynasty, I think."

"I don't get this movie."

"Shh, I can't hear what he's saying."

I still don't get what they were all laughing about in that first scene with the white horse. I think I'm going to cancel my subscription to Netflix if this is the kind of stuff they're showing. I wonder if they have *Ghostbusters*? If they do, I'll consider keeping it. Maybe I'll watch *Ghostbusters* tomorrow. Sigourney Weaver. She was great in *Ghostbusters*. And in *Alien*. They don't make movies like that anymore.

I wonder why Dan keeps changing the direction of my toilet paper roll? I find it switched every time he leaves. Ray always liked it under. And that's the way I like it now. I haven't said anything to Dan. For me it's a way to remember Ray. It wouldn't feel right to have it come down from the top. But it's something to think about. It's like having a Leprechaun in the house. A little bit mischievous but not evil.

"What the hell was that?" I say. "Did you see it? It slithered out from under those rocks. I thought you said this was a comedy."

Dan picked up the remote and paused the video. I'll have to remember to rub it down with alcohol after he leaves.

"Do you want to stop watching it?" he says.

I do, but then what do we do? I wanted a casual relationship. That was okay in the beginning. The night I met him he said if I just wanted someone to go to a bar with, he'd be happy to. But now it seems different. One night we were playing Scrabble and he says, "The loser has to take off a piece of clothing." I always beat him at Scrabble. I don't ask him to take anything off. He was waiting for an answer. Did I want to stop the movie?

"No, that's okay," I say. "I think I get the gist of it. There're these aliens that the rednecks found, and they're being mean. You know, the rednecks are being mean."

"Are we watching the same movie?" Dan says.

"Just start it up again. I'll get it," I say.

I take a sip of wine. My throat feels scratchy. Could I get the virus that quick? When I'm sick with it, maybe all I'll be able to do is lay in bed and watch movies on TV. That's what I used to do when I was a kid. I loved it. Even the commercials were good back then. I stumbled across this one commercial from the sixties when I was googling Harvey Keitel. I loved him in *The Piano*. In the commercial, a blonde lady walks through rooms with Egyptian motifs. The rooms are filled with party people. The blonde chants, "Cigars, cigarettes, Tiparillos..." It's a party in a pyramid. I would love to go to a party in a pyramid. As she makes her way through the party people, she passes two flaming torches like in the old Mummy movies. Mummy movies scared me as a kid. Now they seem corny, like this casket movie.

"Oh yuck, what are they doing to that alien?" I say.

"It looks like they're stretching it," Dan says.

"Yeah," I say.

I decide to ask fewer questions. But is that wise? I should have asked more questions in school. I do Google a lot. Like is Milton Berle still alive? He was on *The Nanny* one time. *The Nanny* is a horrible show, but it puts me to sleep at night. I do like Fran Drescher, though. My phone says Milton Berle died in 2002, and he was five-feet-ten. About five inches taller than me. I like a man to be taller than me. Dan is not. Would anyone name a kid Milton today?

Dan pauses the movie.

"I gotta use the bathroom," he says.

I wonder if Dan is going to change the direction of the toilet paper again? If he doesn't, I might worry that he's depressed. I started worrying about him recently. It was after a Scrabble game. We were playing music from my iPhone onto my Bluetooth speaker. He wanted to hear "I'm So Lonesome I Could Cry" by Conway Twitty. And not just once. He wanted to hear it, like, five times. He even sang along. He can't carry a tune, and sometimes he didn't know what the next word was. I fight my curiosity to go to the bathroom to see if he's changed the direction of the roll. Maybe changing the roll is his way of hinting that he wants to change the direction of our relationship? That might make a good opening scene in a movie. You just see some guy's hands taking the roll off the holder and then slipping it on the other way. The hand takes its time. Maybe even squeezes the roll when it's done. Now that would be a subtle beginning of a movie. Not like this movie.

"How many more minutes left?"

Dan checks the remaining minutes. "About twenty."

I try to concentrate on watching the rest of the movie. I learned what they were laughing about in the beginning. My expectations were higher. My expectations—are they a metaphor for this relationship? Did I expect someone who would intrigue me with toilet paper? Maybe I should be intrigued. His fixation on the TP is kind of cute. That's probably not the best word choice.

"Hey, can you pause it again. Now *I* have to use the bathroom."

I can't wait any longer to see if he did it again. Sure enough, turned around. What could it mean? It's such a subtle thing. Not like laughing at a coffin. I wash my hands. They're so dry. I'm always washing them, so I don't get or give the virus. Which I probably will because he went to that funeral today. I sit down next to him. He smiles.

"That soap smells good," he says.

He traces my ear with his finger and his eyes seem to take in my whole face like he's never seen it before. Then he traces my lips. He leans forward and kisses me softly. Charmin comes to mind. And the big marshmallow man in *Ghostbusters*. And the little guy, Rick Moranis, The Key Master. Somebody sucker punched him while he was walking down the street in NYC the other day. Why would anyone do that? Hmm...Rick Moranis would fit in that coffin.

"Let's finish this movie," I say. And the last scene rolls.

ACKNOWLEDGMENTS

A couple of years ago, my dear friend Karin Pleasant, a social worker and therapist, suggested I should write a volume of short stories themed around what I've gotten wrong in relationships.

"Call it *Red Flags!*" she said.

It was a brilliant idea, but I'd be starting almost from scratch. It would be like saying, "Sure, I'll walk around the world in 80 days with nothing but a backpack, a bag of Twizzlers, and hope in my heart." Sure, I had some pieces kicking around that would fit the theme, but not enough to fill an entire book. Not to mention I had day-job commitments and other creative projects in the pipeline, so I scribbled "red flags" in my *Notebook of Ideas* and left it at that. A few months later, I casually mentioned this idea to publisher Lisa Diane Kastner, Founder and Executive Editor of Running Wild Press. I had no agenda. We were just gabbing during an episode of Running Wild's *Storytellers' Happy Hour*.

"It should be an anthology of authors! When can you start?" she said. Before I knew it, people from all over the country and other parts of the world were submitting drafts. And bam! *Red Flags: Tales of Love and Instinct* was becoming a reality. Lisa K.'s instincts were on point as usual: A group of contributors not only made the process faster, hearing from multiple voices makes it all the richer.

I have thoroughly enjoyed leading this project for the past

nine months. I can't give enough thanks to the amazing contributing authors for trusting me with these nuggets mined from their souls. I looked forward to consulting with them as we developed, shaped, and edited their essays and short stories. In the process, I've made a few new friends. I've definitely expanded my writer's community. And I've honed my skills as a writer and an editor. Even line-by-line editing became like savoring tasty morsels of word flesh. Of course, working on my own pieces was more difficult but provided much-needed nutrition.

People think of "authoring" as a solo sport, but it isn't. I must also thank my support team, including my faithful beta readers, Samuel Fenstermacher, Christopher Gauntt, and new friend Lauren Horn, who provided me with essential feedback on my work. And to my beloved writing cheerleaders, Erin Kelly Pynn, Taryn Bates, Angela Gomez-Holbrook, Sheila Boddeker, Les and Linda Kaye, Terence Hawkins, and Jeff Rogers: You guys are so kind to believe in me. Your faith fuels my courage to navigate the thorny thickets of the writing and editing journey. Many extra helpings of thanks to the inimitable Lisa Kastner who will probably be revealed as the Queen of the Universe someday, which will explain a lot.

ABOUT THE CONTRIBUTING AUTHORS

In order of appearance:

Adrianne Beer received her BFA in creative writing from Bowling Green State University. She is from Yellow Springs, Ohio, and currently lives in Tucson, Arizona, while pursuing a master's degree in library sciences. Her writing can be found in *Moon City Review, Chicago Reader, Entropy,* and elsewhere.

Bobby Rollins is (gratefully) prone to daydreams, some of which he puts into words. He hopes "A Lesson in a Minute," which describes 60 seconds in a couple's relationship and also takes a minute to read, reminds people to value their time and who they share it with. Updates about his writing appear @writerollins on Twitter. P.S. - If the story seems too familiar, consider yourself warned!

Clay Hunt is the author of two poetry chapbooks: "Born Shane" for Two Key Customs and "Young Went the Sun Went Down" for Budget Press. He lives in San Francisco with his partner and pets.

Christopher Gauntt is a jack of many trades including acting, directing, DJ-ing, database programming, dancing, website design, composing, photoshop editing, DIY remodeling, producing, saving the world, and in this instance writing. His level of success and skill in each vary quite widely and are up for constant internal and external debate.

Nazia Kamali is an academic journal reviewer based in Dehradun, a small valley town in the foothills of the Himalayas in India. Her work has been published in *FemAsia, The Whorticulturalist, Rigorous, In Parenthesis, CafeLit Magazine, Bright Flash Literary Review,* and other magazines. When not hunched over the keyboard, Nazia likes to watch birds.

Reuben Tihi Hayslett is a writer, storyteller, and activist. His non-fiction work has appeared in *The Splinter Generation, Oregon Literary Review,* and *The Mary Sue* blog. His fiction work has appeared in the *Surreal South Anthology, transLit magazine* and others. *Dark Corners,* his first short story collection, was named Best of 2019 by Kirkus reviews.

During Benjamin White's 22-year military career, and again when he was earning his MFA from the University of Tampa, he thought he was a poet. But he has since found out that he is not a poet at all. Ben is a witness: what he writes is testimony.

Margo McCall is a Southern California writer whose stories have appeared in *Pacific Review, Howl, Pomona Valley Review, Dash,* and other journals. Her nonfiction has been published in *Herizons, Lifeboat,* and the *L.A. Times.* A graduate of the M.A. creative writing program at CSU Northridge, she lives in Long Beach. For more, visit http://www.margomccall.com.

Wendy Lane is an emerging writer and established visual artist, enchanted by synchronistic events in her life. She retired from a 25-year career in human resources, where she witnessed meaningful coincidences, but confidentiality prevented her from sharing them. She is writing her memoir as a series of personal essays.

Christina Hoag is a former journalist and survivor of an abusive relationship. Her novel *Girl on the Brink* was inspired by her experience and won Best of YA from *Suspense* magazine. A certified domestic violence counselor, she speaks about intimate partner abuse and is a facilitator at support groups. www.christinahoag.com.

Rebecca Rush is a writer and comedian from New London, Connecticut. She hosts *Vulnerability: A Comedy Show,* and she has been featured on *Viceland* and *Funny or Die.* Her work has appeared in *Toho Journal, The Miami New Times, Fodor's Travel, Big City Lit,* and other outlets. She holds a B.A. in English Literature with a Concentration in Creative Writing from the University of Connecticut, where she wrote for *The Daily Campus* and *The Long River Review.* She lives in Los Angeles. Https://rebeccarushcomedy.com

Amara Phoenix is a native Rhode Islander currently living in Georgia. She is a freelance writer and editor, a work-from-home mom, and a bestselling author. When she's not writing, working, or chasing her toddler around, Amara enjoys arts and crafts, reading great stories, and binge-watching absurd reality shows.

When she's not wielding her stethoscope and reflex hammer, Dr. Stella Almazan writes steamy romances about doctors in love and lust. Her life has steadily improved since junior high. She is proud of all her exes, or at least most of them. Always in lipstick and Louboutin's. Even in the shower. Follow her on Twitter @StellaA_Romance.

Joe Beck has written, co-written and ghost-written 12 books, 10 plays and musicals, two of which starred Brian Dennehy and Austin Pendleton. He joined the Yale Writers' Workshop, taught writing at Kingsborough College, and teaches English on Long Island. He's a member of The Authors Guild and The Dramatists Guild.

Phyllis Peterson Levine is in her seventies. She has four children. She waited tables, bartended, worked at a public library and studied painting. She writes short stories and poetry, belongs to a writer's group, and paints. Her work has been published in the *Gordon Square Review*, the *Breakwall*, *Dash* and *Qwerty Magazine*.

ABOUT THE EDITOR

Lisa Montagne, Ed.D., is a writer, artist, college professor, and educational technology specialist from Southern California. She has taught English literature and composition at University of California Irvine, Irvine Valley College, and Long Beach City College. She has been a Carnegie Foundation Research Fellow, and she is an alumna of the Yale Writer's Workshop. Her fiction, creative non-fiction, and poetry have been published by Running Wild Press, the Arroyo Arts Collective, *L.A. Art News Poet's Place, The Ear, The Variant Literature Journal,* and others. She likes performing. She has read her work to audiences in Portland and Tampa, and all over Los Angeles, including at the Beyond Baroque poetry center, at Lummis Day, for the Arroyo Arts Collective, and for Writ Large Press and PenWriter America's series *Drunken Masters.* She is also a Swing, Blues and Argentine Tango dancer. She DJs this music whenever anybody lets her. If you want to see more of her work, keep up with what's new, and maybe see her dressed in costumes, go to lisamontagne.com.

Running Wild Press publishes stories that cross genres with great stories and writing. RIZE publishes great genre stories written by people of color and by authors who identify with other marginalized groups. Our team consists of:

Lisa Diane Kastner, Founder and Executive Editor
Mona Bethke, Acquisitions Editor, RIZE Press
Benjamin White, Acquisitions Editor, Running Wild Press
Peter A. Wright, Acquisitions Editor, Running Wild Press
Rebecca Dimyan, Editor
Andrew DiPrinzio, Editor
Cecilia Kennedy, Editor
Barbara Lockwood, Editor
Cody Sisco, Editor
Chih Wang, Editor
Lisa Montagne, Guest Editor
Pulp Art Studios, Cover Design
Standout Books, Interior Design
Polgarus Studio, Interior Design
Alexis August, Product Manager, RIZE Press
Nicole Tiskus, Product Manager, Running Wild Press
Alex Riklin, Publicity Manager

Learn more about us and our stories at www.runningwild-press.com

Loved this story and want more? Follow us at www.runningwildpress.com, www.facebook.com/runningwildpress, on Twitter @lisadkastner @RunWildBooks